"A prolonge[d] [stay] in my harem [will] provide me with a long-awaited opportunity to teach you what being a woman is all about."

Razul spoke with silken self-satisfaction.

"Your harem?" For the count of thirty seconds Bethany simply stared at him.

"You walk in my world now." Razul issued the reminder with indolent cool. "When you walk from it again you will be a different woman."

LYNNE GRAHAM was born in Northern Ireland and has been a keen Harlequin reader since her teens. She is very happily married to an understanding husband, who has learned to cook since she started to write! Her three children keep her on her toes. She has a very large Old English sheepdog, which knocks everything over, and two cats. When time allows, Lynne is a keen gardener.

Books by Lynne Graham

LYNNE GRAHAM

The Desert Bride

Harlequin Books

TORONTO • NEW YORK • LONDON
AMSTERDAM • PARIS • SYDNEY • HAMBURG
STOCKHOLM • ATHENS • TOKYO • MILAN
MADRID • WARSAW • BUDAPEST • AUCKLAND

ISBN 0-373-11875-9

THE DESERT BRIDE

First North American Publication 1997.

Copyright © 1996 by Lynne Graham.

CHAPTER ONE

THE sheer opulence of Al Kabibi airport stunned Bethany. The acres of glossy marble floors, the huge crystal chandeliers and the preponderance of gold fittings made her blink and stare.

'Pretty impressive, eh?' Ed Lancaster remarked in the slow-moving queue to Visa Clearance. 'And yet five years ago there was nothing here but a set of concrete sheds and an unrelieved view of the sand-dunes! King Azmir pumped the oil but he stockpiled the profits. His tight-fisted attitude caused a lot of resentment, not only with the locals but with the foreign workers as well. Conditions used to be really primitive here.'

The American businessman had joined their flight at a stopover in Dubai. He hadn't stopped talking for thirty seconds since then, but Bethany had been grateful to be distracted from the grim awareness that, had her departmental head not decreed that she centre her research on this particular part of the Middle East, nothing short of thumbscrews and brute force would have persuaded her to set one foot in the country of Datar!

'When King Azmir fell ill the crown prince, Razul, took over,' Ed rattled on, cheerfully impervious to the fact that Bethany had stiffened and turned pale. 'Now he's a different kettle of fish altogether. He's packed fifty years of modernisation into five. He's an astonishing man. He's transformed Datari society...'

Beneath her mane of vibrantly colourful curls Bethany's beautiful face had frozen, her stunningly green eyes hardening to polar ice. All of a sudden she wanted Ed to shut up. She did not want to hear about Prince

Razul al Rashidai Harun. Nor did she have the smallest urge to admit that their paths had crossed quite unforgettably during Razul's brief spell at university.

'And the people absolutely adore him. Razul's like their national hero. They call him the Sword of Truth. You mention democracy and they get *real* mad,' Ed complained feelingly. 'They start talking about how he saved them from civil war during the rebellion, how he took command of the army, et cetera, et cetera. They've actually made a film about it, they're so proud of him—'

'I expect they must be,' Bethany said flatly, an agonisingly sharp tremor of bitterness quivering through her.

'Yes, sirree,' Ed sighed with unhidden admiration. 'Although this divine cult they've built up around him can be painful, he *is* one hell of a guy! By the way,' Ed added, pausing for breath, 'who's coming to collect you?'

'Nobody,' Bethany muttered, praying that the monologue on Razul was over.

Ed frowned. 'But you're travelling alone.'

Bethany suppressed a groan. Actually, she hadn't been alone at Gatwick. A research assistant had been making the trip with her. But, with only minutes to go before they boarded, Simon had tripped over a carelessly sited briefcase and had come down hard enough to break his ankle. She had felt dreadful simply abandoning him to the paramedics but, aside from the fact that she barely knew the young man, work naturally had had to take precedence.

'Why shouldn't I be travelling alone?'

'How on earth did you get a visa?' Ed prompted, suddenly looking very serious.

'The usual way... What's wrong?'

'Maybe nothing.' Ed shrugged with an odd air of discomfiture, not meeting her enquiring gaze. 'You want me to stay with you in case there should be a problem?'

'Of course not, and I see no reason why there should be a problem,' Bethany informed him rather drily.

But there *was*. Ed had just moved off with an uneasy wave when the Datari official scrutinised her visa and asked, 'Mr Simon Tarrant?'

Bethany frowned.

'According to your visa, you are travelling with a male companion. Where is he?'

'He wasn't able to make the flight,' she explained with some exasperation.

'So you are travelling unaccompanied, *Dr* Morgan?' he stressed, with a dubious twist of his mouth, as if he could not quite credit the validity of her academic doctorate. That didn't surprise her. Female children had only recently acquired the legal right to education in Datar. The concept of a highly educated woman struck the average Datari male as about as normal as a little green man from the moon.

'Any reason why I shouldn't be?' Bethany demanded irritably, her cheeks reddening as she was drawn to one side, the embarrassing cynosure of attention for everyone else in the queue.

'Your visa is invalid,' the official informed her, signalling to two uniformed guards already looking in their direction. 'You cannot enter Datar. You will be returned to the UK on the next available flight. If you do not possess a return ticket, we will generously defray the expense.'

'Invalid?' Bethany gasped in disbelief.

'Obtained by deception.' The official treated her to a frown of extreme severity before he turned to address the other two men in a voluble spate of Arabic.

'*Deception*?' Bethany echoed rawly, unable to credit that the man could possibly be serious.

'The airport police will hold you in custody until you depart,' she was informed.

The airport police were already gawping at her with blatant sexual speculation. Even in the midst of her incredulous turmoil at being threatened with immediate deportation, those insolent appraisals made Bethany's teeth grit with outrage. Sometimes she thought her physical endowments were nature's black joke on the male species. With *her* outlook on the male sex she should have been born plain and homely, not with a face, hair and body which put out entirely the wrong message!

'You are making a serious mistake,' Bethany spelt out, drawing herself up to her full height of five feet three inches. 'I demand to speak to your superior! My visa was legitimately issued by the Datari embassy in London—' She broke off as she realised that absolutely nobody was listening to her and the policemen were already closing in on her with an alarming air of purpose.

A sensation new to Bethany's experience filled her. It was fear—sheer, cold fear. Panic swept over her. She sucked in oxygen in a stricken gasp and employed the single defensive tactic she had in her possession. 'I would like you to know that I am a close personal friend of Crown Prince Razul's!'

The official, who was already turning away, swung back and froze.

'We met while he was studying in England.' Her cheeks burning with furious embarrassment at the fact that she should have been forced to resort to name-dropping even to earn a hearing, Bethany tilted her chin, and as she did so the overhead lights glittered fierily over her long torrent of curling hair, playing across vibrant strands that ran from burning copper to gold to Titian in a glorious sunburst of colour.

The official literally gaped, his jaw dropping as he took in the full effect of that hair. Backing off a step, his swarthy face suddenly pale, he spoke in a surge of guttural Arabic to the two policemen. A look of shock swiftly followed by horror crossed their faces. They backed off several feet too, as if she had put a hex on them.

'You are *the one*,' the official positively whispered, investing the words with an air of quite peculiar significance.

'The one what?' Bethany mumbled, distinctly taken aback by the staggering effect of her little announcement.

He gasped something urgent into his radio, drawing out a hanky to mop at his perspiring brow. 'There has been a dreadful, unforgivable misunderstanding, Dr Morgan.'

'My visa?'

'No problem with visa. Please come this way,' he urged, and began to offer fervent apologies.

Within minutes a middle-aged executive type arrived and introduced himself as Hussein bin Omar, the airport manager. His strain palpable, he started frantically apologising as well, sliding from uncertain English into Arabic, which made him totally incomprehensible. He insisted on showing her into a comfortable office off the concourse, where he asked her to wait until her baggage was found. He was so servile that it was embarrassing.

Ironically, the very last thing Bethany had wanted was to draw any unwelcome attention to her arrival in Datar. Suddenly she fervently wished that she had kept her stupid mouth shut. Her reference to Razul had been prompted by a shameful attack of panic. Why on earth hadn't she stayed calm and used logical argument to settle the mistaken impression that there was something wrong with her visa? And why all that silly fuss about the fact that she was travelling alone?

Fifteen nail-biting minutes later the airport manager reappeared and ushered her out... out onto a *red* carpet which had not been in place earlier. Bethany began to get all hot and bothered, her nervous tension rocketing to quite incredible heights. The VIP treatment staggered her. Everybody was looking at her. Indeed it was as though the whole airport had ground to a dead halt and there was this strange atmosphere of what could only be described as...electric excitement.

It *had* to be a case of mistaken identity, Bethany decided, struggling to hold onto her usually bomb-proof composure. Who on earth did Hussein bin Omar think she was? Or did an acquaintance with Razul automatically entitle one to such extraordinary attention at the airport?

What an idiot she had been to claim friendship with him...especially as it was a lie...a really quite blatant lie, she conceded inwardly, grimly recalling her last volatile meeting with the Crown Prince of Datar, slamming down hard on the piercing pain that that memory brought with it. She had had a narrow escape—a damned lucky narrow escape, she reminded herself fiercely. She had very nearly made an outsize fool of herself, but at least *he* had never known that. She hadn't given him that much satisfaction.

A whole column of spick and span policemen were standing to attention on the sun-baked pavement outside. Bethany turned pale. The heat folded in, dampening her skin beneath the loose beige cotton shirt and serviceable trousers she wore. Her discreet little trip to Datar had gone wildly off the rails.

'Your escort, Dr Morgan.' Hussein bin Omar snapped his fingers and a policeman darted forward to open the door of the waiting police car.

'My escort?' Bethany echoed shakily just as a young woman hurried forward and planted an enormous bunch of flowers in her startled hands. As if that were not enough, her fingers were grasped and kissed. Then for a split second everybody hovered as though uncertain of what to do next.

'*Allah akbar*...God is great!' the airport manager suddenly cried. Several other excited male voices eagerly joined him in the assurance.

At that point Bethany simply folded backwards into the police car. The whole bunch of them were crazy! Instantaneously she scolded herself for the reflection. As an anthropologist trained to understand cultural differences, such a reflection ill became her. As the car lurched into sudden motion and the driver set off a shrieking siren to accompany their progress she told herself to be calm, but that was difficult when she noticed the two other police cars falling in behind them.

Common sense offered the most obvious explanation. Hussein bin Omar had been appalled by the mistake over her visa because she had claimed that she knew Razul. In short, this outrageous fuss was his attempt to save lost face and simultaneously demonstrate his immense respect for the Datari royal family. That was why she had been supplied with a police escort to take her to her hotel outside the city. All very much over the top, but then this was *not* England, this was Datar—a feudal kingdom with a culture which had only recently begun to climb up out of the dark ages of medievalism.

She closed her eyes in horror as her driver charged a red light, forcing every other vehicle to a halt. Fearfully lifting her lashes again, she gazed out at the city of Al Kabibi as it sped by far too fast. Ultra-modern skyscrapers and shopping malls mingled with ancient, turquoise-domed mosques, the old and the new coexisting side by side.

As it left the lush white villas of the suburbs behind, the broad, dusty highway forged a path through a landscape of desolate desert plains. Bethany sat forward to get a better view of the fortress-like huge stone walls rising out of the emptiness ahead. Her driver jabbered excitedly into his radio while endeavouring to overtake a Mercedes with only two fingers on the steering wheel.

Bethany was on the edge of her seat, praying. And then, without any warning at all, the car swerved off the road outside the fortress and powered through a set of enormous turreted gates. A clutch of robed tribesmen suddenly appeared directly in their path. They were brandishing machine-guns. The driver jumped so hard on the brakes that Bethany was flung along the back seat, and then she heard the splintering crack-crack of gunfire and threw herself down onto the floor, curling up into as tight a defensive ball as possible.

The car rolled to a halt. She stayed down, trembling with fear, wondering if the driver had been shot but not prepared to raise her head until the bullets stopped flying. The door clicked open.

'Dr Morgan?' a plummy Oxbridge voice enquired expressionlessly.

Bethany peered up and met the politely questioning gaze of a dapper little Arab gentleman with a goatee beard.

'I am Mustapha—'

'The g-guns...?' she stammered.

'Merely the palace guards letting off a little steam. Were you frightened? Please accept my apologies on their behalf.'

'Oh...' Feeling quite absurd, Bethany flushed and scrambled out of the car; only then did alarm bells start ringing. 'The *palace* guards?' Wide-eyed, she stared at the older man. 'This isn't my hotel?'

'No, indeed, Dr Morgan. This is the royal palace.' He permitted himself a small smile of amusement. 'Prince Razul requested that you be brought here without delay.'

'*Prince Razul*?' Bethany repeated in a strangled voice, but Mustapha had already swept off towards the arched and gilded entrance of the vast sprawling building ahead, clearly expecting her to follow him.

The airport manager must have contacted Razul about her arrival, Bethany registered in horror. But why on earth would Razul demand that she be brought to the palace? After the manner in which they had parted two years earlier he could not possibly wish to see her again!

Lifelong conditioning to the effect that he was every woman's fantasy did not prepare an Arab prince for the shattering experience of having his advances rebuffed. By the end of their last, distressing encounter Bethany had been left in no doubt that Razul had been very deeply offended by her flat refusal to have anything to do with him.

Yet she had planned what she would say to him in advance, employing every ounce of tact at her disposal. She had known the strength of his pride. She had gone to great lengths in her efforts to defuse a volatile situation gently. Her face shadowed now, the cruel talons of memory digging deep. Razul had unleashed his temper and goaded her into losing her head. She wasn't proud of the derision with which she had fought back but he had been tearing her in two. She had been fighting for her own self-respect . . . why not admit it?

As she followed the older man into a huge, echoing hall lined with slender marble columns she was in a daze. Her exotic surroundings merely increased the sensation. Tiny mosaics were set into wildly intricate geometric patterns in shades of duck-egg green and ochre and palest blue on every inch of the walls and ceiling. The effect was dazzlingly beautiful and centuries old. A tiny sound jerked her head.

A giggle . . . a whisper? She looked up and saw the carved *mishrabiyyah* screens fronting the gallery suspended far above her. Behind the delicate yet wholly effective filigree barrier she caught flutters of movement, fleeting impressions of shimmering colour and then a burst of girlish laughter, excited whispers emerging from far more than one female voice and then swiftly stifled. A drift of musky perfume made her nostrils flare.

A tiny window onto the outside world for the harem? Bethany froze and turned white, a terrible pain uncoiling inside her. The thesis which had earned her both her doctorate and her current junior lectureship at a northern university had been on the suppression of women's rights in the Third World. *This* was not the Third World but, even so, the dreadful irony of her almost uncontrollable attraction to Razul had boiled her principles alive two years ago. Her colleagues had laughed their socks off when he'd come after her...an Arab prince with two hundred concubines stashed in his harem back home!

'*Dr Morgan*!' Mustapha called pleadingly.

Numbed by the onslaught of that recollection, Bethany moved on again. At the far end of the hall two fierce tribesmen stood outside a fantastically carved set of double doors. They wore ceremonial swords but carried guns. At a signal from Mustapha they threw back the doors on a magnificent audience room. The older man stepped back, making it plain that he was not to accompany her further.

At the far end of the room sunlight was flooding in from doors spread back on an inner courtyard. It made the interior seem dim yet accentuated the richness of its splendour. Her sturdy leather sandals squeaked on the highly polished floor. She hesitated, her heartbeat hammering madly against her ribcage as she stared at the shallow dais, heaped with silk cushions and empty. But a terrible excitement licked at her every sense and she felt it even before she saw him—that frightening mix of craving and anticipation which for the space of several weeks two years earlier had made her calm, well-ordered life a hell of unfamiliar chaos.

'Dr Livingstone, I presume?'

She jerked around, that honey-soft accented drawl sending a quiver down her taut backbone. Her breath shortened in her throat. Thirty feet away on the threshold of the courtyard stood the living, breathing embodiment of a twentieth-century medieval male—Razul al Rashidai Harun, the Crown Prince of Datar, as uncivilised a specimen of primitive manhood as any prehistoric cave would have been proud to produce.

'All that outfit lacks is a bush hat. Did you think you were coming to darkest Africa?' Razul derided lazily, and her serviceable clothing suddenly felt like foolish fancy dress.

She couldn't take her eyes off him as he walked with cat-like fluidity towards her. Breathtakingly good-looking... terrifyingly exotic. With those hard-boned, hawkish features, savagely high cheek-bones and that tawny skin he might have sprung live from some ancient Berber tapestry. He was very tall for one of his race. Sheathed in fine cream linen robes, his headdress bound by a double royal golden *iqual*, Razul gazed down at her with night-dark eyes that were as hard as jet.

It took enormous will-power to stand her ground. Her mouth went dry. Razul strolled calmly around her, for all the world like a predator circling his kill. It was not an image which did anything to release her tension.

'So very quiet,' Razul purred as he stilled two feet away. 'You are in shock... the barbarian has at last learnt to speak proper English...'

Bethany lost every drop of her hectic colour and flinched as though he had plunged a stiletto between her ribs. 'Please—'

'And even how to use your dainty Western cutlery,' Razul imparted with merciless bite.

Bethany dropped her head, anguish flooding her. Did he really think that such trivia had mattered? Her heart had gone out to him as he'd struggled, with all that savage pride of his, to fit into a world which his suspicious old father had denied him all knowledge of until he'd reached an age when the adaptation was naturally all the more difficult to make.

'But the barbarian did not learn one lesson you sought to teach,' Razul murmured very quietly. 'I had no need of it for I know women. I have always known women.

I did not pursue you because I was prompted by my primitive, chauvinistic arrogance to believe myself irresistible. I pursued you because in your eyes I read blatant invitation—'

'No!' Bethany gasped, galvanised into ungluing her tongue from the roof of her dry mouth.

'Longing...hunger...*need*,' Razul spelt out so softly that the hairs prickled at the nape of her neck. 'Those ripe pink lips said no but those emerald eyes begged that I persist. Did I flatter your ego, Dr Morgan? Did playing the tease excite you?'

Appalled that he appeared to recall every word that she had flung at him, Bethany was paralysed. He had *known*. He had known that on some dark, secret level she'd wanted him, in spite of all her protestations to the contrary! She was shattered by the revelation, had been convinced that her defensive shell had protected her from such insight. Now she felt stripped naked. Even worse, Razul had naturally interpreted her ambivalent behaviour in the most offensive way of all. A *tease*...? Sexless, cold and frigid were epithets far more familiar to her ears.

'If you believe that I misled you, it was not intentional, I assure you,' Bethany responded tightly, studying her feet, not looking at him, absolutely forbidding herself to look at him again, not even caring how he might translate such craven behaviour. Maybe she owed Razul this hearing. He was finally having his say. Two years ago his fierce anger had not assisted his efforts to express himself in her language.

The silence smouldered. She sensed his frustration. He wanted her to fight back. Funny how she knew that, somehow understood exactly what was going through that innately devious and clever brain of his. But fighting back would prolong the agony... and she *was* in agony, with the evocative scent of sandalwood filling her nostrils and the soft hiss of his breathing interfering with her concentration. It took her back—back to a terrifying time when her safe, secure world had very nearly tumbled about her ears.

'May I go now?' She practically whispered the words, so great was her rigid tension.

'Look at me—'

'No—'

'Look at me!' Razul raked at her fiercely.

Bethany's gaze collided with vibrant tiger-gold eyes and she stopped breathing. The extraordinary strength of will there mesmerised her. Her heartbeat thudded heavily in her eardrums. All of a sudden she was dizzy and disorientated. With a sense of complete helplessness and intense shame, she felt her breasts stir and swell and push wantonly against the cotton cups of her bra as her nipples pinched into tight little buds. Hot pink invaded her pallor but there was nothing she could do to control her own body. The electrifying sexual charge in the atmosphere overwhelmed her every defence.

Razul dealt her an irredeemably wolfish smile, his slumbrous golden eyes wandering over her, lingering on every tiny hint of the generous curves concealed by her loose clothing. Then, without warning, he stepped back and clapped his hands. The sound was like a pistol shot in the thrumming silence.

'Now we will have tea and we will talk,' Razul announced with an exquisite simplicity of utter command that made Bethany recall exactly *who* he was, *what* that status meant and *where* she was. This rogue male was one step off divinity in Datar.

Bethany tensed and jerkily folded her arms. 'I don't think—'

Three servants surged out of nowhere, one with a tray bearing cups, one with a teapot, one with a low, ebonised, brass-topped table.

'Early Grey...especially for you,' Razul informed her, stepping up on the dais and dropping down onto the cushions with innate animal grace.

'Early Grey'? She didn't correct him. The oddest little dart of tenderness pierced her, making her swallow hard. She remembered him surreptitiously shuffling that 'dainty Western cutlery' he had referred to at a college dinner. Then she locked the recollection out, furious with herself. Miserably she sank down onto the beautiful carpet, settling her behind onto another heap of cushions, but her disturbing thoughts marched on.

She had been infatuated with him—hopelessly infatuated. Every tiny thing about Razul had fascinated her. She had been twenty-five years old but more naïve in many ways than the average teenager. He had been her first love, a crush, whatever you wanted to call it, but it had hit her all the harder because she hadn't been sweet sixteen with a fast recovery rate. And she had been arrogant in her belief that superior brainpower was sufficient to ensure that she didn't succumb to unwelcome hormonal promptings and immature emotional responses. But *he* had smashed her every assumption about herself to smithereens.

'There was a bit of a mix-up over my visa at the airport...I wouldn't have mentioned your name otherwise,' she heard herself say impulsively, and even that disconcerted her. She was not impulsive, but around Razul she was not herself. The china cup trembled betrayingly on the saucer as she snatched it up to occupy her hands and sipped at the hot, fragrant tea.

'Your visa was invalid.'

'I beg your pardon?' Bethany glanced up in astonishment, not having expected to hear that nonsensical claim again.

'Young women are only granted visas under strict guidelines—if they are coming here to stay with a Datari family, can produce a legitimate employment contract or are travelling with a relative or male colleague,' Razul enumerated levelly. 'Your visa stated that you would be accompanied. You arrived alone. It was that fact which invalidated your documentation.'

Bethany lifted her chin, her emerald-green eyes flashing. 'So you discriminate against foreign women by making lists of ridiculous rules—'

'Discrimination may sometimes be a positive act—'

'Never!' Bethany asserted with raw conviction.

'You force me to be candid.' Brilliant dark eyes rested on her with impatience, his wide mouth hardening. 'An influx of hookers can scarcely be considered beneficial to our society.'

'Hookers?' Bethany repeated in a flat tone, taken aback.

'Our women must be virgin when they marry. If not, the woman is unmarriageable, her family dishonoured. In such a society the oldest profession may thrive, but we did not have a problem in that field until we granted visas with too great a freedom.'

'Are you trying to tell me that I was mistaken for some sort of tart at the airport?' Bethany gritted in a shaking voice.

'The other category of female we seek to exclude I shall call "the working adventuress" for want of a more acceptable label.'

'I'm afraid I don't follow,' Bethany said thinly.

'Young women come here ostensibly to work. They flock to the nightclubs that have sprung up in the city. There they dress, drink and conduct themselves in a manner which may be perfectly acceptable in their own countries but which is seen in quite another light by Datari men,' Razul explained with a sardonic edge to his rich vowel sounds. 'A sizeable percentage of these women do not return home again. They stay on illegally and become mistresses in return for a lifestyle of luxury.'

'Really, I hardly look the type!' Bethany retorted witheringly, but her fair skin was burning hotly. 'And, fascinating as all this is, it's time that I headed for my hotel.'

'Lone women in your age group are not currently accepted into our hotels as guests.'

Bethany thrust a not quite steady hand through her tumbling hair. 'I beg your pardon?'

'No hotel will offer you accommodation when you arrive alone.' His strong dark face utterly impassive, Razul surveyed her intently. 'Had I not brought you to the palace you would now be on a flight back to the UK.'

'But that's ridiculous!' Bethany suddenly snapped, her nervous tension splintering up through the cracks in her composure. 'It's hardly my fault that my assistant broke an ankle before we boarded!'

'Most unfortunate.' But he said it with a faint smile on his beautifully moulded mouth, and his tone more than suggested that he was not remotely interested in the obvious fact that her planned stay in Datar had now run into petty bureaucratic difficulties, which she was quite sure he could brush aside... should he want to.

Bethany pushed her cup away with a very forced smile, behind which her teeth were gritted. 'Look... this is an important research trip for me—'

'But then you take all your work so seriously,' Razul pointed out smoothly.

Her facial muscles clenched taut. 'I am here in Datar to research the nomadic culture,' she informed him impressively.

'How tame...'

'Tame?' Bethany echoed in shrill disconcertion, having assumed that his own cultural background would necessarily prompt him to treat the subject with appropriate respect.

'I have read your paper on the suppression of women's rights,' Razul murmured very softly.

'You've read my paper?' Bethany found herself gawping at him.

'And, having done so, intend to generously offer you research in a field which could make you famous in the academic world when you return to the West.' Burnished golden eyes suddenly struck hers with ferocious force.

'What field?' Bethany queried, a frown-line dividing her brows as she shifted uneasily on the cushions, instinctively reacting to the humming tension in the air.

Razul unleashed a predatory smile upon her. 'A way of life never before freely opened to the scrutiny of a Western anthropologist. I feel remarkably like Santa Claus.'

'Excuse me?' The atmosphere was suffocatingly tense. Bethany scrambled upright and involuntarily backed away from the controlled menace that emanated from Razul in vibrating waves.

'A prolonged stay in my harem will not only provide you with liberal scope for academic research, it will provide me with a long-awaited opportunity to teach you what being a woman is all about,' Razul told her with silken self-satisfaction.

CHAPTER TWO

'YOUR harem?' For the count of thirty seconds Bethany simply stared at Razul, her bright green eyes open to their fullest extent. Then she visibly bristled, her naturally sultry mouth compressing into a thin, unamused line. 'Very funny,' she said flatly, but there was an unevenness to her response as she fought against the giant tide of bitterness threatening to envelop her.

'You walk in my world now.' Razul issued the reminder with indolent cool. Veiled dark eyes slid over her in an all-encompassing look that was as physical as a caress. 'When you walk from it again you will be a different woman.'

Her aggressive stance—feet apart and arms taut—quivered as a tide of fury surged through her, leaving her light-headed. 'If you look at me like that once more, so help me I will knock your teeth down your throat!' Bethany blistered back at him.

A scorching smile slashed his hard mouth, perfect white teeth flashing against his golden skin. He surveyed her with intense pleasure. 'My father said... "Is this woman worth a diplomatic incident?" If he saw you now, truly he would not have asked such a question.'

'What do you mean, "worth a diplomatic incident"?' Bethany demanded, her voice half an octave higher.

'Sooner or later you will be missed,' Razul pointed out gently. 'Questions will be asked, answers must be given. Our ambassador in London will be called to the Foreign Office. But I suspect it will be many weeks before we reach that stage—'

'The Foreign Office?' Bethany shook her head as though to clear it, a daze of utter disbelief beginning to enfold her.

'You see, you have so few people in your life to notice that you are missing. You write to your mother only once a month. You communicate with your father not at all. Your sole close friend is currently enjoying an extended honeymoon in South America—her fall from grace in allowing a man into her life very probably loosened the ties of that friendship. As for your academic colleagues...?' Razul enumerated these facts in the same calm, measured tone, as though he was well aware of her growing incredulity. 'This is the long summer vacation. I doubt if they will be expecting to hear from you. I find your life of isolation a sad testimony to your wonderful Western civilisation.'

The pink tip of Bethany's tongue crept out to moisten her dry lower lip. Shock was reverberating through her in debilitating waves. 'How...how do you know all these things about me?' she whispered jerkily.

'An investigation agency.'

'You put a private investigator on me? But when? You didn't even know I was *coming* to Datar!'

'Did I not? A liberal endowment to your university ensured your eventual arrival—'

'I b-beg your pardon?' Bethany stammered, a painful throb of tension beginning to pulse behind her browbone.

'Why do you think your superiors insisted that you base your research on Datar?'

'The nomadic tribes here have not suffered the same level of exposure to the modern world as in other countries,' she informed him harshly, her hands clenching in on themselves.

'True...but who suggested the subject of your research?'

Bethany went rigid. The idea had come down from on high. It had not emerged from the anthropology department itself. Indeed there had been resentful mutters to the effect that she must have admirers in high places because such research opportunities abroad were, due to a shortage of finance, currently at an all-time low.

'I'm building your university a brand-new library,' Razul shared with her gently. 'And my carefully chosen British representative, who stressed his special interest in Datar and also mentioned how very impressed he was by a series of lectures you gave last year, insisted on absolute and complete anonymity in return for the endowment.'

Bethany was starting to tremble. Without a flicker of remorse he was telling her that she had been lured out to Datar on false pretences. 'No...I don't believe you...I *refuse* to believe you!'

'I have known the date of your arrival since you applied for your visa. I was not, however, prepared for you to arrive alone at the airport,' Razul conceded wryly. 'Or for the subsequent furore over your visa, but your solitary state has worked to my advantage. You now have no companion to raise the alarm...and I have you in my possession that much sooner.'

'You have not got me in your possession, you maniac!' Bethany snatched up her duffel bag and stalked to the exit doors. 'I've listened to this nonsense long enough as well!'

'You are prepared to endure bodily restraint?'

'Meaning?'

'Without my permission you are not allowed to leave the palace.'

'Nobody *allows* me to do anything...I do what *I* want to do!' Bethany spat back at him, and jerked at the ornate handles with furious fingers. 'And I am returning to the airport!'

'If you force my men to put their hands upon you they will be severely embarrassed that you should invite such an indignity... but they will not flinch from their duty,' Razul warned.

The doors sprang open. Instantly the two guards outside spun round and faced her, yet they did not look directly at her and she remembered how at the airport, after she had mentioned Razul, the male eyes had swiftly averted from her as she'd passed. It was an insult for an Arab man to stare openly at an Arab woman who was not of his family... but she was *not* one of their women. Such pronounced respect ironically sent a shudder down her backbone, and the mere concept of instigating a pointless struggle with those fierce-looking men made her cringe. In one violent movement of frustration Bethany thrust the doors shut again.

'If you don't let me out of here I'll scream!' she hurled down the length of the room at Razul.

'It will only make your migraine worse.'

How did he know that she got migraine headaches? How did he know that she could already feel the first dismaying signs of an attack?

'You think I won't scream, don't you? You think I'm so damned impressed by your utterly ridiculous threats and your blasted throne room, I haven't got the bottle!' Bethany fired off at him, shaking all over with rage.

'"The bottle"?' A frown-line divided his winged ebony brows as he rose fluidly upright and began to move towards her.

'Stay away from me...I'm *warning* you!' On the edge of hysteria for the very first time in her life, Bethany threw back her shoulders and screamed. It hurt her ears, it hurt her throat, it hurt her head. But what shook her even more was the reality that nobody came running to see what was amiss.

'Ask yourself what happiness your life in the West has brought you,' Razul urged her softly as he moved towards her. 'You work relentless hours. You drive yourself like a mouse on a treadmill and deny yourself every feminine pleasure.'

'I am extremely happy!' Bethany launched back rawly, her back pinned to the doors. 'I'm totally fulfilled by my work.'

'Being totally fulfilled by me will be infinitely more satisfying. It will release all that pent-up tension—'

'The only way I am likely to release my pent-up tension at this moment is by physically attacking you...if you don't keep your distance!' Bethany swore, fighting against the increasing pounding of the building migraine, feeling her skin dampen, her stomach lurch. 'Now maybe you think this little power game of yours is amusing but it has gone far enough...do you hear me? I want transport back to the airport *right now*!'

'If I gave you what you say you want you would regret it for the rest of your life,' Razul asserted wryly. 'I will not permit you to make so foolish a decision.'

'Back off, Razul!' As he got too close Bethany took a defensive leap along the wall and saw swimming spots in front of her aching eyes, but she fought her own weakness to the last ditch. 'The joke has gone stale. You cannot possibly intend to keep me here against my will. I couldn't possibly be your type—'

'I have catholic taste—'

'Intellectually I find you—'

'A challenge? When you have rested for a while you will feel more adjusted to the wonderful change in your circumstances. No longer are you alone—'

'I *like* being alone!' Bethany screeched.

'You are afraid to share yourself—'

'I am not sharing anything with you!' It was a cry of despair. Suddenly, without warning, she snapped, the rigidity going out of her, hot tears burning her eyes, making her cover her rapidly working face with shaking hands.

A pair of strong hands inexorably peeled her off the wall which was supporting her. 'No!' she gasped in horror.

An even stronger set of arms relentlessly swept her off her feet. Her head was spinning in a cartwheel of fire. Her gaze clashed with glittering gold eyes set between lush ebony lashes longer than her own, and a stifled moan of mingled pain and defeat was dredged from her.

'Stop fighting me.'

'Put me down,' she sobbed weakly.

'Shush...' he whispered softly, soothingly. 'Surrender can be the sweetest pleasure of all for a woman. You were born to yield, not to fight.'

She closed her water-clogged eyes, feeling too ill to try and struggle against overwhelming odds. *Overwhelming odds*...Razul in a nutshell, she reflected wretchedly. Two years ago she had blown every penny she'd possessed on a trip to Canada to stay with her aunt to escape him. Like a drug addict she had suffered withdrawal symptoms of sleepless nights, lost appetite, moodswings and, worse, the frightening conviction that she had a streak of masochism more than equal to anything that her martyred mother had ever displayed in her dealings with her wandering husband.

Razul was carrying her and without any apparent effort. The scent of him so close washed over her...clean, warm, intensely male. They had never been *this* close before. But she had wondered—oh, yes, she had wondered what it would feel like to be in his arms. Now it had been thrust on her when she was defenceless and, worst of all, she *liked* it, she registered in horror—*liked* the fact that he had taken charge, liked the soft, rich feel of his robes against her cheek, the raw male strength of him, the steady thump of his heartbeat. A sob that had nothing at all to do with her migraine escaped her.

A clamour of anxious female voices chattered in Arabic as she was laid down on a bed. A cool hand rested

on her forehead. Razul. A part of her wanted to retain
that contact and that made her feel worse than ever. He
lifted her up. 'Drink this...'

Her medication was in her bag but she drank the herbal
concoction, lay back, weak as a kitten, and momentarily
lifted her heavy eyelids. Two young women were kneeling
on the carpet several feet from the bed and they both
wore fixed and matching expressions of frantic concern
and unholy fascination. Melodrama was born in Arabia,
she thought helplessly.

'The doctor is coming.' Razul smoothed the fiery
tangle of curls off her damp brow. His hand wasn't quite
steady. 'Close your eyes; relax,' he instructed in that
dark, deep voice of his. 'Tension must increase the pain.'

Relax? A spasm of anguish snaked through her. He
had brought her to the harem. Those had to be *his*
women watching her. Wives, concubines— Oh, dear
heaven, what did it matter what they were? she asked
herself bitterly. He was still one man with two hundred
young and beautiful women at his disposal—*gifts* from
his father's adoring subjects.

Datar had made an official complaint to the British
government when a certain notorious tabloid had spilt
what the Dataris considered to be very private beans to
an agog British public. Diplomatic relations had been
cut off for six months. Contracts which should have gone
to British firms had suddenly been awarded elsewhere.
Since then the media had been tactfully silent about the
Crown Prince of Datar's exotic sex life. Not a murmur
had appeared in print since those revelations two years
earlier.

Razul had been shattered when she'd dared to fling
those same facts in his teeth—so outraged, so furious,
so nakedly incredulous that any woman should dare even
to mention such an unmentionable subject, never mind
berate him with a personal opinion of his morals, that
he had forgotten every word of English that he *did* have,

slamming back at her in his own language before he'd
stormed out, leaving her sobbing and empty and bitter
as gall.

In a haze of surprising drowsiness and broken shards
of memory Bethany drifted at first, like a boat on a
storm-tossed sea, but the boat slowly came into the calm
of harbour, drawn there by the cool, strong fingers reas-
suringly linked with hers. Feeling inexpressibly relaxed,
she slid into a deep, dreamless sleep.

Bethany wakened to the sound of chattering birds and
stretched languorously. Her dark lashes lifted and she
saw not a ceiling but a dome of incredibly beautiful
stained glass far above her. She sat up with a stifled gasp.
There was another shock awaiting her. She was not alone.
Three brightly smiling young girls were kneeling in total
silence on the carpet.

'You are awake, *sitt*.' One of them rose gracefully and
shyly lifted gorgeous almond-shaped eyes to hers. Her
slender body was garbed in a colourful, tight bodice and
swirling skirt, her feet shod in embroidered slippers, gold
jewellery tinkling with her every movement. 'I am
Zulema. We have been chosen to serve you. Many wished
for this honour but only I speak English. Prince Razul
say I speak English very good...is good enough?' she
checked in sudden dismay, the query undoubtedly
prompted by the fact that Bethany was gaping at her.

Bethany snatched in a gulping breath, striving to get
a grip on herself as she took in the fabulous room and
its alarming unfamiliarity, then glanced down and
fingered the equally unfamiliar filmy white silk gown
she was mysteriously clad in. 'You speak wonderful
English, Zulema,' she mumbled weakly.

'I will run a bath for you, *sitt*. You must long to be
fresh. You had a very long journey, but it is so thrilling,
I think, to fly on a plane. Once I travelled to London
with Princess Fatima—' Zulema's animated little face

abruptly clouded and she dropped her shining dark head as if she had dropped a clanger.

Fatima... who was Princess Fatima? Razul's sister, mother, aunt... wife? Bethany knew nothing about his family.

As Zulema hurriedly pressed the other girls into activity Bethany absorbed their unhidden high spirits and the rather discomfiting way they kept on stealing fascinated glances at her. Were they maids or was their connection with Razul of a more intimate nature? After all, every one of them was wearing enough gold jewellery to sink the *Titanic*. Dear God, Razul had put her in his harem just as he had promised. And he had *drugged* her to keep her here last night!

What had been in that seemingly innocuous drink that she had trustingly taken from his hand? She had never managed to sleep through a migraine before. Whatever he had given her had knocked her out cold. She had slept through what remained of yesterday late into a new day. And right now she was in shock—so much shock that her brain was traumatised. The sound of running water came noisily through a door now flung wide. In a sudden motion Bethany slid from the bed. Zulema gasped and surged to proffer slippers as if the wonderful, silk-soft rug were insufficient to protect her feet.

'Please...' Please leave me alone, she wanted to plead, but when Zulema looked up at her with a horribly embarrassing look of near-worship, as if she were some sort of goddess instead of a perfectly ordinary woman the same as herself, Bethany was struck dumb.

'We will bathe you, *sitt.*'

Bethany, who found even communal changing rooms a mortification, was appalled by the suggestion. Fighting to hide the fact, she murmured tightly, 'You don't need to serve me, Zulema.'

'But you are the one... you must be served,' Zulema protested anxiously.

The one *what*? Bethany almost screamed, recalling that same phrase from the airport but restraining herself. 'Where I come from,' she said stiltedly, 'we do not share bathrooms.'

Zulema giggled and delightedly shared this barbaric desire for privacy with her companions. Bethany took advantage of the huddle to slide past them into the bathroom and close the door. The ultra-modern appointments were reassuring. The bedroom, furnished with antique cedarwood inlaid with silver, had given her the disorientating impression that she had been snatched back to the time of Sheherazade. Peeling off the gown, she climbed into the bath which had been run for her, but she sat rigid in the richly scented water like a puritan invited to an orgy, furiously washed herself and clambered back out again as fast as she possibly could.

By the time she had finished with Razul he wouldn't be able to get her back to the airport quickly enough! Was he crazy? Did he really imagine that he could make a prisoner of her? *Of course*, he could not seriously mean to try and keep her here by force. But everything he had told her the previous night flooded back to her—the endowment to the university... the strict anonymity demanded... her own surprise, as a junior member of the department, when she had been offered the research trip.

She emerged from the bathroom wrapped in towels. 'Where are my clothes?'

With pride Zulema indicated the fabulous heap of jewel-coloured silks now strewn over the bed.

'*My* clothes... my suitcase,' Bethany extended tautly.

Neither was forthcoming. Ignoring her audience, Bethany flicked open chests and closet doors. *Nothing*, not a stitch of her own clothing in sight! She wanted to stamp her feet and scream with temper, and it must have showed because Zulema and her helpers looked worried sick, as if any sign of dissatisfaction on her part was likely to bring punishment down on their unprotected heads.

'OK... I'll wear this stuff. Choose something for me,' Bethany invited grudgingly.

Smiles broke out again like magic. Zulema extended an emerald-green silk caftan edged with gold, and a filmy pair of lace briefs and matching bra, the likes of which Bethany had never harboured in her plain white cotton underwear drawer. A flush of increasing rage mantling her cheeks, she dressed and stood at the mirror with a silver-backed brush, yanking it brutally through her long, wild mane of tangled curls.

'I have displeased you, *sitt*?' Zulema pressed in a small, tearful voice. 'Why you not like my help?'

Bethany felt all mean and small-minded and contemptible and handed over the brush, taking a seat on a divan. How the heck could you force the principle of equality on someone when equality was neither acknowledged nor desired?

'Such glorious hair. I have never seen such wonderful hair,' Zulema sighed, delicately teasing out each snarl with reverent fingers. 'It *is* the colour of the setting sun, just as was said.'

'Said by whom?'

Zulema giggled shyly. 'Prince Razul's guards, they talk... It is forbidden that they talk, but men, they gossip too. A long time ago we hear about the English lady with the hair of glorious colours... soon all our people know and talk and the King, he got very angry indeed to hear the whispers about his beloved son. Ah... the English breakfast is here!' Zulema carolled excitedly as the door opened.

What kind of whispers? Bethany wanted to know as she stood up, but Zulema threw wide yet another door, revealing a dining table and chairs. 'Just like home,' she told Bethany as a procession of servants bearing trays followed in her wake.

Open-mouthed, Bethany stared as the trays were unloaded and the lids on the metal dishes were lifted one by one. Fruit juices, cereals, toast, croissants, breakfast rolls, wheaten bread and every possible kind of preserve. Fried eggs, boiled eggs, scrambled eggs, *even* coddled eggs. Kippers, devilled kidneys, beef sausages, fried bread, tomatoes and French toast. It was lunchtime but she was receiving breakfast.

Zulema pulled out a chair and Bethany collapsed down onto it, surveying the banquet before her. She was hungry but never in her life had she seen such a spread for one individual. The entire table was covered.

'You like?'

'I'm very impressed.' Her voice wobbled in the presence of such shamelessly conspicuous consumption.

'Prince Razul bring in chef from Dubai. If you not like his cooking, he go back,' Zulema informed her cheerfully.

Razul had hired a chef specifically to cook Western food for *her*? Heavens, did he actually think that she would be staying long enough for it to matter? Bethany took a deep breath, feeling more and more as though she was existing in some outrageous fantasy world, aeons removed from her own life of quiet, sensible practicality.

She was finishing her tea when Zulema approached her again.

'The Prince...he say he meet with you now,' Zulema whispered, as if she were setting up an incredibly exciting romantic assignation.

Bethany stood up and straightened her narrow shoulders with Amazonian spirit. 'And don't spare the horses.'

'The horses?'

'Never mind.'

*   *   *

The palace was an astonishingly large building. It rambled all over the place in a hotchpotch of corridors, screened galleries and sunlit courtyards.

At the head of a superb marble staircase Zulema abruptly halted and drew back several steps. 'We must wait, *sitt*.'

Bethany looked over the wall down into the magnificent courtyard below, but her attention had not been attracted by the lush selection of tropical plants and the beautiful playing fountains. It was Razul she saw, his luxuriantly black, slightly curly hair gleaming like raw silk in the strong sunlight...and then the woman, sobbing and clutching frantically at his ankles.

'We go for walk, *sitt*,' Zulema urged uncomfortably.

'No, thanks.' In all her life Bethany had never seen a woman humiliate herself to such an extent. She was appalled. She needed no grasp of Arabic to interpret that distraught voice, that subservient posture and the passionate intensity with which the poor woman was hanging onto him.

Razul hissed something in his own language and literally stepped over her. As she attempted to follow him he snapped his fingers furiously at a cluster of servants cowering in a corner. Within seconds they were rushing to lift the woman from the ground and hurry her away through one of the archways off the courtyard.

'Who is that woman?' Bethany whispered.

'The Princess Fatima,' Zulema muttered thinly. 'Prince Razul take only one wife. Always he say that...only the one.'

Bethany's stomach lurched sickly. Perspiration broke out on her brow. So Razul was married. Dear heaven, that tormented woman was his wife, and it did not take great imagination to comprehend the source of her hysteria, did it? Razul had brought another woman into the palace and the poor creature was quite naturally distraught. The sheer cruelty of his behaviour devastated

Bethany. He was every inch the savage, despotic Arab prince, who believed his own desires to be innately superior to any mere female's wants and needs.

In a tempest of pain she refused to acknowledge Bethany descended the marble stairs. Razul swung round, his starkly handsome features flushed and still set with cold anger and hauteur. And then, as his stunning golden eyes settled on Bethany, the tension went out of him. A dazzling smile completely transformed his strong dark face.

That smile hit her like a shock wave, made her steps falter and her heart give a gigantic lurch behind her breastbone. For a split second she was hurled back two years to the evening they had first met. She had been coming out of the library. He had been leaning against the bonnet of his Ferrari, surrounded by gushing female students, every one of whom had been blonde and not known for her inhibitions with men. And then he had looked up and focused on Bethany and perceptibly stilled, treating her to a narrowed, intent stare before suddenly flashing that spectacularly glorious smile. Riveted to the spot, she had dropped her books.

But *not* this time, she swore to herself, despising her own shameful susceptibility and the disturbing emotions and responses which could block out every rational thought.

'I've always been told that the Arab male cherishes and protects the women in his family,' she shot at him in stark challenge, 'but report really doesn't match reality, does it? The Princess Fatima does not appear to qualify for even an ounce of your respect.'

His smile vanished as though she had struck him. A dark rise of blood delineated his hard cheek-bones. 'You saw...?'

'I saw,' Bethany confirmed shakily.

'I am disturbed that you should have witnessed so distressing a scene but, in honour, I may not discuss it with you,' Razul delivered in a grim undertone.

Bethany turned away. She could not bear to look at him. So he had that much decency—a tiny kernel of loyalty to his wife. And he was profoundly embarrassed that she had seen that distasteful encounter... amazing. It was almost as though he expected her to pretend that these other women did not exist in his life. Concubines *and* a wife.

Yet she had never been able to hate him properly for his lifestyle. Just as she was a product of her world, he was a product of his. Nor was she foolish enough to imagine that Datar was the only country in the world where concubines were kept. It was not a subject referred to; it was a subject politely ignored lest people in high places be offended. And she had often wondered how many Western males could truthfully say that, given the same opportunity and society's silent blessing, they too would not indulge in the freedom of such sexual variety.

'Did you sleep well?'

A laugh that was no laugh at all bubbled in her throat. 'You should know... you drugged me—'

'You were in great pain. I could not bear to see you suffer,' Razul imparted tautly, on the defensive. 'A sleeping potion allowed you to rest.'

A sudden unbearable sadness swept over her. She found herself sinking down on the stone edge of a fountain, and she let her fingers trail restively in the water. 'And how do you answer the kidnapping and imprisoning charge?'

'You gave me no other option.'

Bethany breathed in deeply and looked at him where he stood, brushing aside the disturbing realisation that in the superbly tailored dove-grey suit which outlined his broad shoulders, narrow hips and long, lean legs he

looked achingly familiar to her. On the outside touched
by Western sophistication, she thought painfully, on the
inside not touched at all, and not about to apologise for
it either.

'You know I won't let you get away with a cop-out
like that,' she whispered.

'Cop-out?' Razul queried flatly, standing very tall and
taut.

'An evasion.' She guessed that the women in his life
let him off the hook every time he smiled, and then
doubted if he even had a passing acquaintance with being
pinned between a rock and a hard place by her sex.
Fatima had been crawling round his feet like a whipped
dog, not standing up to him like an equal.

Pain trammelled through her afresh. Was that what
had attracted Razul to a woman outside his own
culture...to her? Her spirit, her independence? In Datar
even the male sex walked in awe of Razul al Rashidai
Harun. One day he would be their king.

'You cannot seriously intend to imprison me here—'

'It does not have to be a prison. Give me your word
that you will not attempt to escape and you may roam
free.'

'Something of a contradiction in terms.' Unwarily she
connected with smouldering golden eyes intently pinned
to her and her throat closed over. Why am I talking to
him so calmly instead of screaming at him? she wondered. Her own pain had risen uppermost, swallowing
up the anger. Worse still, there was a treacherous part
of her that greedily cherished every stolen moment in
his company. The knowledge filled her with a deep,
abiding shame.

'*Je te veux...*' he had said two years ago. 'I want you.'

'*Tu es à moi,*' he had purred like a sleek jungle cat.
'You are mine.'

Temptation—sinful, sweet, soul-destroying...

'You are an educated man,' Bethany muttered not quite steadily.

'On the surface. Don't flatter me,' Razul said with sudden harshness. 'I know your opinion of me. My father allowed thousands of Datari men to attend British and American universities over the last two decades. He did this only because it became clear to him that our country would become totally dependent on foreign workers if he did not encourage our young men to seek education and technological training in the West. But he would not permit me to enjoy a similar experience.

'I am well aware that reading many books and spending a short spell at university does not make me an educated man...especially not in the eyes of a woman who has a string of letters after her name and many academic accomplishments.'

In the hot, still air the tension pulsed and throbbed, beating down on her from the electric force of his challenging gaze. He possessed one very powerful personality, one very volatile temperament which was also unashamedly emotional, but you were never in any doubt of the ferociously strong will that lay behind it all. But only now did she register the innate humility with which he viewed himself on an intellectual level, and that discovery pained her and made her want to put her hands round the throat of his obstinate old father, who had denied his own son what he freely gave to his subjects.

Her throat thickened. 'Razul, nobody who has seen what you have managed to achieve here in Datar over the past five years could possibly think you anything other than an educated man.'

'I make use of many advisors from all levels of our society. I will not tolerate nepotism, for placing the unfit in authority is the curse of the Arab world. I seek to liberalise our culture for the benefit of our people...but I know what you think, *aziz*, as I say this.' He sent her a dark, level appraisal. 'You think how can I talk of liberalisation and then steal a woman.'

'I'm well aware that stealing women is an element of the tribal culture,' Bethany informed him in a frozen voice. 'But—'

A brilliant smile crossed his beautifully shaped mouth. 'It is not a crime as long as the woman is treated with respect and honour,' he smoothly inserted.

Bethany bent her fiery head, staggered to find herself on the brink of laughter. When it suited Razul, he was wondrously, deviously simplistic, and her mere admission that woman-stealing was a tradition practised for centuries in his culture delighted him in so far as he saw that as ample justification for his conduct.

'But naturally the marriage must take place within a short space of time,' Razul remarked softly. 'It is expected.'

Her head flew back, shimmering green eyes fixing on him in unconcealed shock.

The silence stretched, taut as a rubber band, between them.

With a muffled expletive in Arabic Razul took a long stride forward and then stilled, sheer incredulity sufficient to match her own flashing across his staggeringly handsome features. 'In the name of Allah, *aziz*...surely you could not think I would insult you with anything less than an offer of marriage? Last night...was this why you panicked?' he demanded starkly, and reached for her hands to tug her relentlessly upright. 'I brought you here to become my wife!'

His *second* wife. In a storm of outrage Bethany looked at him in absolute disbelief, and then she tore her hands violently free and fled.

CHAPTER THREE

PASSING beneath the nearest archway, Bethany found herself in an elaborate reception room. Fighting for self-control, she closed her eyes. 'Prince Razul take only one wife. Always he say that... only the one.' Zulema's explanation for Fatima's distress returned to her now. Seemingly Razul was now prepared to break that promise to his wife, and in a society where he was all-powerful what could the wretched woman possibly do? Presumably she could live with her husband's other female diversions but felt both betrayed and threatened by the prospect of another woman acquiring the same status as herself.

Marriage... woman-stealing was all above board as long as you offered holy matrimony to satisfy the conventions. A strangled laugh, empty of amusement, escaped her. Little wonder she had been treated like royalty at the airport, little wonder she was being waited on hand and foot. Everybody *but* her had expected marriage to follow her arrival!

A polygamous marriage. The teachings of the Koran taught that a Muslim was entitled to up to four wives at any one time. In a lifetime he could get through many more than that number, if he so desired, by the judicious use of divorce. The ex-wives, of course, had to be liberally provided for. One of the reasons why polygamy was becoming less prevalent in the Arab world was the sheer expense of maintaining multiple families. But Razul was fabulously rich.

Oddly enough it had never occurred to her two years ago that Razul might already be a married man. The tabloid hadn't picked up on that... but then maybe he had not been married then. She raised trembling hands to her stiff, cold face.

'Why are you distressed?' It was a ferocious demand, raw with a frustrated lack of comprehension. 'Perhaps you are ashamed to have misjudged me so badly,' Razul suggested with savage bite. 'This is not Bluebeard's castle. I am not some filthy rapist who would force his unwanted attentions upon an unprotected woman! Do you seriously believe that my father would have agreed to me bringing an Englishwoman here had I not intended to marry her? Do you think us savages?'

Bethany wanted to howl with hysterical laughter and slap him hard to express her emotions at one and the same time. 'The Princess Fatima?' she whispered chokily.

'Fatima must learn to adjust. This is not my problem,' Razul dismissed, slashing the air with an angry and imperious hand. 'I do nothing to be ashamed of. I have waited two long years for you and she is well aware of this...'

Bethany gazed at him in horror. 'Your compassion is overwhelming,' she muttered sickly.

'Compassion is not infinite... no more is tolerance. Why do you treat me to this response?' Razul launched at her. 'It makes no sense!'

'Last night...' Bethany was struggling to think straight while dimly wondering what he could possibly find incomprehensible about her response. Dear heaven, did he fondly imagine that a *marriage* proposal two years ago would have been sufficient to change her attitude towards him? Did he think that she would have fallen gratefully at his feet in welcome? And when he now offered what he no doubt saw as the ultimate of honours, did he think that that would magically overcome her resistance?

'*What* last night?' Razul appealed with driven emotion.

'You kept on saying that when I went *back* to my world... You weren't thinking of marriage then!' she reminded him.

Razul set his incredibly eloquent mouth into a grim line. 'I was making it clear that were you to be unhappy I would set you free. I would give you a divorce, but *only* after you had given our marriage a fair and reasonable trial.'

Inside herself, beyond her angry disbelief, she hurt. She turned her head away. She would never have married Razul in any circumstances. Even if he hadn't had Fatima and those other women, she reflected painfully, she still would have said no. Marriage was not for her and would never be for her. She had seen far too much of the misery of marriage while she had been growing up, and, beyond that again, the even greater misery of a cross-cultural union.

Even so, she was shattered by the idea that Razul would *want* to marry her. Two years ago he had wanted an affair...and she wouldn't have been his first affair on campus—no, far from it! She might not have met Razul until his second term but she had *heard* about him...oh, boy, had she heard! His fame had gone before him.

Razul had flung himself with immense enthusiasm into a world where women were willing to share his bed without the smallest commitment on his part. Blessed by gorgeous good looks, charming broken English intermingled with fluent French, enormous wealth and the certainty that he would one day become a king, Razul had hit the female student body much like a winning lottery ticket blowing in the wind, hopefully to be captured by the most determined of his many admirers. A kind of communal hysteria had reigned in his radius, she recalled painfully.

'I could never marry you,' Bethany informed him tightly.

'Do not say never to me... I will not accept it.'

'I insist that you call a car to take me to the airport!'

'I refuse.' Razul sent her a raw, shimmering glance of gold.

'You are thinking of the loss of face...' Bethany assumed, suddenly wishing that she did not understand his culture to the degree that she did. If he had informed his family that he intended to marry her and she refused, it would be a humiliation for him. A public humiliation. There was undoubtedly not a woman in Datar who would deny herself the great honour of becoming one of his wives.

'Again you go out of your way to insult me.' Razul slung her a look of wrathful reproach, his hands clenching into fists by his sides. 'What lies between us runs too deep to rest on something so superficial as what you term a "loss of face"!'

Bethany was paper-pale, but rigid with a strength of will every bit as unyielding as his own. 'There is nothing between us and there never will be. You *must* accept that. In my opinion my sole attraction in your eyes is the fact that I said no two years ago! Your ego can't live with the startling concept that there exists one woman in the world who wants nothing to do with you!'

'When you speak such barefaced lies I lose all patience with you!' Razul blazed at her with such explosive suddenness that she flinched. He closed the distance between them in one long, panther-like stride and reached for her. 'These lies are naked provocation!'

As he hauled her into his arms Bethany stiffened in shock. Glittering golden eyes roamed over her startled face with a scorching heat that made her skin tauten over her bones. 'You burn for me as I burn for you—'

'*No!*'

'I saw your hunger last night.' Razul lifted a shapely hand and knotted long fingers very slowly into the fiery tumble of her long hair. 'I hold you and your heart beats as madly as that of a gazelle hunted down in the desert. It beats for me and for no other man. Yet I have never touched you,' he breathed, in a throaty undertone of frustration which sent taut quivers rippling down her rigid spine. '*Never* ... How many men in your world could say that of the woman they longed to possess? How many men would treat you with such unquestioning respect?'

His thumb was rubbing against the lobe of her ear. A tiny little shiver ran through her, fracturing her breathing. Eyes as keen as those of a hawk in flight scoured her hectically flushed face, beating down on her with merciless insight. She trembled, a whirling tide of dizziness assailing her, the hiss of her indrawn breath shatteringly loud in the stillness. 'Razul, I—'

'You trust me to observe the boundaries...why?' Razul demanded roughly, yet the long forefinger he lifted to trace the tremulous fullness of her lower lip was tormentingly gentle, brushing across the tender skin with innate eroticism. 'In the mood I am in your trust is a step too far. Perhaps I have been too honourable...I made it too easy for you to drive me away in England, but I will not make it easy *this* time.'

'Let go of me,' Bethany mumbled thickly, her slender length slipping from rigidity into sudden, shivering weakness as that expert finger slid against her trembling mouth. A tide of sexual awareness strong enough to wipe out her every defence was infiltrating her now.

'Have other men not held you...touched you?' Unhidden anger harshened his rich dark voice. 'Why do you expect me to be different?'

Her breasts rose and fell, heavy, swelling, her nipples peaking inside the gossamer-fine covering of her bra. A languorous heat was uncoiling between her thighs, making her shift like a cat arching its back in the sunshine, but in the depths of her unthinking mind lurked an equally animal fear of her own responses. '*Don't*!'

'But your eyes say *do*... and if I had behaved as a man of your world you would not have shunned me two years ago. I allowed you to stay free,' Razul intoned with mesmeric intensity. 'Do you know why an unmarried woman is not left alone with a man in Arabia? A man is expected to sin and a woman is deemed too weak to resist temptation, for was she not fashioned to be the greatest pleasure of a man's existence? As you will be mine, heart, soul and body... for that I promised myself in England and I will fulfil that promise more sweetly than you can believe...'

'Airport!' Bethany said jerkily, as if he had yanked a string and that was the best her blitzed reasoning powers could come up with by way of a contradiction.

Razul laughed softly. A lean hand sank to the shallow indentation of her spine and pressed her closer as he slowly lowered his arrogant dark head. 'The image of a jet taking off... the heavens opening as the gates to your secret garden... most fitting, but then you are an extraordinarily sensual woman,' he murmured thickly. 'Did I not sense that from the first?'

A violent shudder snaked through her as his warm breath fanned her cheek. He took her mouth in a hot, hungry surge of possession and dragged her down so deep and so fast into a world she didn't know, she was lost. He prised her lips apart with the tip of his tongue and probed the moist, tender interior that she instinctively opened to him. With a strangled moan Bethany caught fire in a surging blaze of passion.

Excitement, raw, wild and overpowering, took her by storm. With every fevered kiss she hung on the edge of desperation for the next, crushing her thrumming body into the hard, lean heat of him for the closeness that every fibre of her femininity greedily craved. Her hands swept up and found his broad shoulders, dug in there briefly to trace the hard stretch of his taut muscles beneath the rich fabric of his jacket before convulsively

linking round his strong brown throat, her seeking fingers
flirting deliciously with the luxuriant black hair at the
nape of his neck.

With a stifled groan he suddenly tightened his arms
around her as he lifted her up against him, kissing her
breathless with an intense urgency that stoked the flames
of her arousal to unbearable heights. She clutched at
him, knotting her fingers into his thick, silky hair, for
he was the only stable influence in a whirling vortex of
violent passion. He muttered something rough against
her swollen mouth, momentarily stiffening as if to
withdraw, but she held him there, kissed him again with
the same raw, answering hunger that he had chosen to
awaken in her.

He drew her down, down onto softness and support,
crushing her quivering length just as swiftly beneath his
superior weight. As he sealed his long, muscular body
to hers the heat of desire washed over her with such
strength that she burned, her hips arching up, her legs
torturously confined in the clinging cloth of her caftan.
His hand closed round her breast and she gasped,
shocked by sensation, instinctively straining her swollen,
seeking flesh upwards to meet that possessive hold.

Razul dragged his lips free of hers, staring down at
her with blazing golden eyes, his cheek-bones harshly
delineated beneath his smooth, sun-bronzed skin as he
snatched in a ragged breath. He loosened his grip, ran
a torturous fingertip over the shamelessly distended
nipple poking against the fine silk barrier, sending fire
shooting to the very centre of the throbbing ache between her thighs. She closed her eyes in an agony of
excitement and shuddered as if she were in a force-ten
gale.

'I cannot do this,' Razul breathed with subdued ferocity, abruptly pulling back from her and yet carrying
her with him, his strong hands grasping her arms as he
tugged her upright again. 'To do this is to shame you,

and I will not have regrets between us. You will come
to me as my bride or you will not come at all!'

He settled her down like a doll onto a low divan.
Bethany didn't know what had happened to her. Her
entire body felt as though it had acquired a life of its
own, and right now it was screaming with a clamouring
dissatisfaction which was cruelly unwelcome. In short,
she ached—ached for a physical completion which she
had never desired in her life before—and she sat there,
struck dumb by sheer horror as her mind fumbled up
out of the darkness of complete shut-down to reason
again. And yet she did not want to think...

'I always knew that your desire would match mine,'
Razul confessed with rough satisfaction. 'Now you must
acknowledge that too and be grateful that my control is
greater...though in truth it was not that which restrained my ardour...the doors are ajar.'

Be grateful? Bethany sat there in the burnt ashes of
self-discovery, her fire ignobly doused by a bucket of
cold reality. She had never endured such a tumult of
agonised emotion. She was seized by shame and loathing
for both herself and for him. 'Fatima...' she whispered
strickenly, and hung her head, wondering how any man
could possibly reduce her to such a level of selfish,
mindless insanity.

'What has she to do with us?' Razul demanded with
savage impatience. 'Do not speak her name to me again!'

How *could* he talk like that? Nausea stirred in her
cramping stomach. She was so unbearably ashamed of
her own behaviour. How could she have forgotten Fatima
for one moment? How could she have? Feverish tears
scorched her lowered eyelids as she scrambled upright.
'You must let me go!'

'You are the most stubborn woman I have ever met,'
Razul condemned harshly, frustratedly. 'Why can you
not talk to me? Why do I *still* meet the same silence?

Are you so prejudiced against my race that you cannot listen to your own heart?'

The charge of racial prejudice hit her like a final intolerable blow. Bethany shot him a look of bitter reproach and took off as if all the bats in hell were on her trail.

Strangled sobs were clogging her throat when she found Zulema waiting for her on the gallery above. She rammed them back with every atom of fierce discipline that she possessed and lifted her head high, concealing the agonising strain threatening to tear her wide open.

How dared he bring her here . . . how dared he subject her to such an intolerable situation? He was stirring up feelings from the past—angry, disturbing emotions which she had thought had been laid to rest. It was her pride which was hurting, she told herself. Her stupid, childishly irrational crush on him two years ago was a memory which now made her cringe. That she should be forced back into contact with him again was naturally a nightmare of mortification. It was like returning to the scene of the crime.

Back in her palatial suite of rooms, she paced the floor, too frantically strung up to sit down. She knew what was *really* wrong with her. She was still reeling with shock from the physical response that he had extracted from her, was barely able to credit that that wanton woman in his arms had been her. After all, that kind of physical stuff had always left Bethany cold. Even in the grip of infatuation she had assumed that the reality of any closer contact with Razul would pretty much match her distasteful grappling experiences with other men. But *now* she had learned the shattering extent of her own vulnerability and she was disgusted with herself.

How could she have allowed him to touch her like that...how could she have? Maybe it was her own fault, she thought grimly. She was a twenty-seven-year-old virgin . . . but that had never bothered her, never caused her the least discomfiture or regret until *he'd* landed in her radius! She had never felt the slightest bit repressed until *he'd* awakened those grossly uncomfortable feelings of curiosity and awareness two years ago. Only now did she face the fact that she must have denied the physical side of her nature for far too long when a *married* man could put his hands on her and make her behave like a sex-starved wanton!

In two long years Razul had not forgotten her...why? Good old-fashioned lust and the challenge that she had foolishly made of herself. In England Razul had laid siege to her as though he had been conducting a military manoeuvre. She had been deluged with flowers and gifts of expensive jewellery. A couple of months on campus had taught Razul exactly what most Western women expected from an Arab prince. She had returned the jewellery. But when she had failed to be impressed, had he given up and returned to more appreciative admirers? *No way.*

Whatever Razul had to fight for was one thousand times more desirable to him than what came easily. His shrewd intelligence and resourcefulness had come into play as he'd focused more on the kind of woman she was. An exquisite Persian kitten had landed mysteriously on her doorstep. When she had worked late at the library an anonymously prepaid taxi would be waiting outside to take her home again. He had invited her to the opera and to external lectures instead of discos and nightclubs.

And she had kept on saying 'no', 'sorry', 'no' and 'no' over and over again, pleading pressure of work and other social engagements, never once saying, until the very last, 'I'm not interested...I'm not attracted to you...I don't like you,' because those had been lies— the most outright lies she had ever told. And the terrible thing had been that Razul had known that she was lying and had been bitterly angered by her refusal to recognise

the fierce attraction between them. That was why he had
not forgotten her.

She covered her face with unsteady hands, feeling as
though her whole being was in wild turmoil, and it terrified her. How the heck could he do this to her? What
was it about him that he could *still* get to her to such
an extent? She was appalled by her own inability to think
straight. And when she looked back on the conversation
that she had had with him in that courtyard she was
even more unnerved by the peculiarities of her own
conduct. She had sat there trailing her fingers in that
fountain and actually *talking* to him! Was that rational
behaviour? Why hadn't she demanded her freedom in
terms which could not be ignored? Why hadn't she
threatened him...got him by the throat...and told him
that he was a kidnapper?

Her head was spinning over these inconsistencies.
Somehow she had to make Razul let her go. She focused
on that dark, driven frustration of his last words to her.
Surely his own instincts would do the persuading for
him? Whatever response Razul had expected to his proposal, he had not received it. Indeed, she had the extraordinary suspicion that Razul had actually believed that
she might be flattered that he should have gone to such
incredible lengths to bring her to Datar, especially when
his manoeuvres were accompanied by the assurance of
wholly honourable intentions.

Honourable? The human male didn't come much more
basic than Prince Razul al Rashidai Harun. She had
severely dented his ego when she'd rejected him outright
in England. So in that immeasurably arrogant, obstinate way of his he had put together what he saw as a
winning package which no woman in her right mind
could conceivably refuse...marriage! He was insane.
Apart from the obvious fact that she absolutely loathed
him, could he not see the vast gulf of understanding and
cultural indoctrination which separated them...why did

he refuse to see it? She wanted to scream and tear her hair out at the same time.

Without warning the bedroom door burst open. Startled, Bethany focused on the ravishingly beautiful brunette standing on the threshold. She was wearing a fabulous lemon brocade suit which shrieked designer sophistication. Huge, lustrous brown eyes set above exotically tilted cheek-bones zeroed in on Bethany, and the pouting red mouth twisted into a vicious line of rage.

'I am Fatima...'

Bethany was paralysed by a clutch of emotions, but horror rose uppermost. Razul's wife. She couldn't have opened her shocked mouth had her life depended on it. She wanted a large dark hole to sink into.

Fatima surveyed her with raw loathing. 'Hair the colour of carrots!' she spat. 'You ugly English bitch!'

This was no poor, weeping, tormented woman, Bethany noted dumbly. In fact, there wasn't a sign that there had *ever* been tears on that remarkably beautiful face. There was a look of such simmering violence and uncontrollable fury that Bethany actually feared a physical assault.

'You think you can take my place...but let me tell you what Razul will give you!' Fatima ranted, stalking forward. 'He'll give you a fake marriage, not the real thing! *Mut'a*...you're so clever, you should know what *mut'a* means. It is a marriage contract for a day, a week, at most a month or two. It doesn't even require a divorce! Men use it to take the woman they want and then toss her aside again!'

Bethany had only a very vague idea of what *mut'a* entailed, and even though it was totally irrelevant she found herself thinking that she had not known that Dataris recognised temporary marriage contracts. Such agreements could satisfy the strict conventions of a society which condemned sexual relations outside the bonds of matrimony. Sin and shame were thus avoided.

Even a one-night stand could be deemed respectable if it observed the rules.

'Fatima—' Bethany began painfully.

'You are shocked!' Fatima rejoiced in shrill interruption. 'You are also stupid! King Azmir would never permit his son to marry a Western woman under any other circumstances!'

'Fatima...please forgive me for the pain I have caused you just by being here,' Bethany pleaded tautly, no longer able to meet the brunette's eyes, so deeply ashamed did she feel, even though she had not asked for the ghastly situation she now found herself in. 'And please believe that I have no desire to marry your husband—'

'*My*—?' Fatima screeched.

'Razul refuses to allow me to leave the palace!' Bethany didn't want any more distasteful screeching and rushed in to interrupt.

'Refuses to allow...?' Fatima sounded dazed, which Bethany could well understand since the woman obviously believed that she was here by free choice. 'You do not want to be here? You do not want to marry Razul? I cannot believe this—'

'Nevertheless it is the truth!' Bethany broke in fiercely. 'I want absolutely nothing to do with him. I had no idea that Razul intended to bring me here or even that he was a married man—'

'Ah...' Fatima's pouting little mouth slowly set into a coldly malicious smile of comprehension. '*This* is why you wish to leave him.'

Bethany flushed hotly. 'Only *one* of the many reasons,' she stressed curtly.

'If you truly wish to leave, *I* can easily get you out of the palace,' Fatima informed her, with a glinting little smile. 'The old women in our family still hide themselves behind the veil when they go out. Who could tell what lies beneath the *chador*?'

'I would be very grateful for your help—'

'I will make the arrangements.'

The brunette yanked open the door and loosed a terse volley of Arabic on Zulema, who was waiting outside. The girl cowered and then fell down on her knees, trembling as if she was terrified. With a most unlikeable air of malicious satisfaction Fatima walked out, leaving Bethany alone. What a bitch, Bethany couldn't help thinking, and then she bent her head, asking herself what right she had to stand in judgement. This was not her world—oh, no, indeed, this was not her world, and the sooner she was out of it again, the happier she would be, she told herself fiercely.

Bethany was lying on a divan, glancing abstractedly through a glossy magazine, when she caught a disturbing glimmer of movement in the reflection of a tall mirror to one side of her and turned her head. Shock shrilled through her, her breath escaping her in a sudden hiss as she shot to her feet.

'Try not to scream...' Razul sent her a smile of raw amusement that acknowledged her astonishment. 'These are the women's quarters, and in honour of your reputation I should not be here—'

'Damn right... you shouldn't be!' Bethany spluttered breathlessly. 'How the hell did you get in here?'

'SAS training. I crossed the roof and dropped down onto the balcony.'

She hadn't heard a sound but then he had always moved with the silent prowl of a natural predator. 'You could have broken your stupid neck!' she snapped. 'What do you want?'

'Obviously I should have come at night and brought the chocolates,' Razul sighed with lazy mockery. 'You do not have a romantic bone in your body, Dr Morgan.'

Bethany flinched, her facial muscles tightening.

'But we can work on that problem together. You ask why I am here... and I am tempted to ask, Are you joking?' Razul drawled. 'You retreated at speed from a serious discussion.'

'I made my feelings quite clear,' Bethany said shakily.

Razul shoved his hands into the pockets of his well-cut trousers and elbowed back his jacket, displaying the solid breadth of his chest and the taut flatness of his stomach, not to mention the now sleekly defined lines of his lean, muscular thighs. Colour ran up into her cheeks, her tongue sliding out to moisten her dry lips in a darting motion.

Eyes of vibrant gold flicked to her, catching her in the act of appraisal, and his innately sensual mouth curved with instantaneous recognition. Dense ebony lashes screened his eyes down to a smouldering sliver, returning her gaze with earthy masculine amusement. 'When you have not got the restraint to prevent yourself from visually ravishing me, how am I to accept these extraordinarily confused feelings you insist that you have made clear?'

Another tide of hot pink surged up beneath her fair skin. 'I was not—'

'You were,' Razul slotted in silkily. 'You watch me as I watch you. Green light...but then red stop-light. It infuriates me...and right at this moment it makes me want to throw you down on that bed and release that promise of passion again, until you sob against the exquisite torture of my lovemaking and beg me for that ultimate fulfilment. After that experience I seriously doubt that you will again offend my hearing with the lie of your lack of interest.'

Standing there, wordlessly entrapped by the dark, intensely passionate lure of him, Bethany was pretty doubtful too. Her colour fluctuating wildly, she backed away from him, her skin hot and tight as it stretched over her quivering nerve-endings in involuntary response to the electrifying sizzle of raw sexual awareness now churning up the atmosphere.

'I don't deny that...that there's a certain attraction between us,' she heard herself confess between gritted teeth, feeling herself under threat and ready to make that one concession if it held him at bay.

'This is very sudden,' Razul derided.

'I b-beg your pardon?'

'You finally admit the truth, but it is no longer enough.'

Rampant frustration filled her. 'What point is there, then, in admitting such a truth?'

'A crumb from the table when I want the whole loaf?' His sensual mouth hardened as he sent her a swingeing look of scorn. 'I want everything you have to give...and then more. I do not stand at your door like a humble suitor. I will take what you seek to deny me. I will possess you as you have never been possessed, and when it is over you will never forget me... *this* I promise you!' he swore in a biting undertone that sent tiny chills of fear rippling down her rigid spine.

She had thought that finally acknowledging that attraction would satisfy him. Instead, for some reason, that admission had inflamed him. 'What could we possibly have in common?' she demanded starkly.

'You are innocent indeed if you do not know that there are more exciting things between a man and a woman than similarity.'

'No! I know all about *that* kind of excitement!' Bethany slung the assurance at him in disgust as she spun away, her entire body thrumming with the strength of her emotional turmoil. 'And it's not for me.'

She was painfully well acquainted with the sort of violent sexual attraction which could spring up between radically different people. It had happened between her parents. Her irresponsible, utterly self-centered and vain father had waltzed in and out of her childhood as and when it had suited him: when another relationship had broken down, when he'd been short of money, out of

work or simply wanting home comforts for a while. He
had been far too clever to get a divorce. And her loving
mother had kept on opening the door, forgiving, trusting,
always ready to hope again that *this* time he would be
different and he would stay.

Time and time again Bethany had been urged to make
her father feel at home, keep him happy, act as if he
were a permanent fixture rather than someone just
passing through. Even remembering that period of her
life made Bethany's stomach churn sickly. She had
promised herself then that, unlike her mother, she would
find her fulfilment in a career. She would be independent and self-sufficient. She would never, ever make
herself vulnerable by building her life round some man.

'Who taught you such a lesson?' Razul probed.

Dragged back in a shaken state from her own painful
memories, Bethany focused on him, feeling that wild,
crazed lurch of her every sense and hating him for having
the power to do that to her. It was terrifying to feel that
she was no longer in control of her own responses.

'Twenty-seven years old and you behave like a mixed-
up teenager... Why do you fight me like this?'

'Because this is an impossible attraction... why the
hell can't you see that and accept it?' she practically
screamed at him from her turmoil of ragged nerves, on
the edge of a breakdown. 'Why couldn't you just leave
me alone? Don't you ever think about anybody but
yourself? Luring me out here and subjecting me to
this nightmare is positively sadistic! *You...are...
hurting...me!*' And then her voice broke off in horror
that she should have revealed that reality.

His veiled dark eyes were impenetrable. 'You hurt
yourself, *aziz*. When you gain the courage to see that,
perhaps you will also have the grace to be grateful that
I chose to give you a second chance.'

Her mouth wobbled below her outraged emerald-green eyes. 'A second chance?' she parroted in a strangled voice, scarcely believing her ears.

'Which you have yet to prove yourself deserving of. Did I not desire you so greatly, I would have set aside all thought of you a long time ago,' Razul delivered harshly.

'I hate your guts... can't you see that?' she blistered back at him rawly.

'What I see is... fear.'

'Fear?'

'There's nowhere to run this time. And when you retreat I advance. You are losing ground fast.'

'Are we playing war games now?' she derided shrilly.

'This is no game.' Razul glanced with irritation at his watch. 'I have a meeting—'

'You *have* to let me go!' Bethany asserted, incredulous at the lack of effect she was having on him.

He took a step closer. Bethany leapt back. He laughed with genuine amusement, tremendous charm in that sudden, spontaneous smile. Approaching her, he lifted a hand and curved long, caressing fingers to the taut line of her jaw. 'I anticipate a long, hot summer in which you will change from the woman you are into the woman you could be... You will not want me to let you go,' he forecast with immense confidence.

'Don't touch me!' Bethany jerked her head back out of reach of that disturbingly intimate caress, trembling all over, feeling cornered and menaced and infuriated by the unfamiliar sense of inadequacy that he was evoking within her.

In answer Razul knotted his fingers into a hank of curling hair and brought his mouth down on a collision course with hers. Almost incoherent with rage, she tried to evade him but he held her fast, forced her to be still and kissed her, and she went down into the heat of hell-fire and damnation without a murmur, electrified by the force of her own hunger. He pressed her back against the wall, both of his hands linking fiercely with hers, and kissed her breathless, crushing her ripe mouth under his until her senses swam in hot, drowning pleasure.

'I will count the hours until I have you in my bed...' Razul confessed raggedly, and withdrew from her.

Wildly dizzy and dazed, she stayed upright on the power of shock alone. She opened her heavy eyes. He was gone. She slid down the wall like a boneless rag doll and shivered and shook, devastated by what he could make her feel, emotionally and physically drained by her own turmoil. What the hell was she going to do if Fatima didn't help her? How long would it take the brunette to make what she had called 'arrangements'?

But Fatima reappeared within half an hour of Razul's exit. Again the door opened without any prefatory knock. A veiled shape stood on the threshold. Fatima was cloaked in the voluminous folds of the *chador* which screened the female form from head to toe, and it was indeed an effective disguise. Bethany only recognised her visitor by her acid-yellow court shoes. A bundle of cloth was tossed at her feet.

'Hurry...the car is waiting for us!' Fatima hissed impatiently.

'Now?'

'Have you changed your mind?'

'Of course not!' Bethany gasped.

Her heart beating like a drum, she pulled on the tent-like *chador*.

'Conceal your hands in the pockets,' Fatima instructed. 'And keep your head down and do not speak.'

There was no sign of Zulema in the corridor outside. Bethany found it incredibly difficult to walk with all that fabric flapping around her. When I get home I'll laugh about this, she promised herself, but she knew that she wouldn't... Indeed, all she could think about was the fact that she would never, ever see Razul again, which made her furiously, bitterly angry with herself.

CHAPTER FOUR

FATIMA led Bethany out to a dusty, cobbled yard
bounded by a long line of garages. A Range Rover was
sitting there with the engine already running. Bethany
clambered into the back like a drunken sailor in her
companion's graceful wake. The car roared off and,
mindful of the driver, Bethany continued to keep her
head bent. Half an hour would take them to the airport—
maybe a little more, she conceded, fingering the weight
of her shoulder bag beneath the *chador*. She had her
passport but no flight ticket... Hell, a seat on a flight
anywhere would do as long as it got her out of Datar!

The car lurched and jolted, the engine thundering.
They were moving at considerable speed. Bethany finally
emerged from her reverie to notice that the drive was
taking a lot longer than she had expected. Twisting, she
peered out of a side-window and was astounded to realise that the four-wheel drive was crossing a flat salt
plain and there was no sign of a road or, indeed, of any
other traffic. Her lips parted. 'Where—?'

A startled gasp of pain escaped her as a set of pincer-
like nails bit into the back of her exposed hand. Her
head spun round. Her eyes collided with seething brown
ones and she gulped. She dug her hand shakily into the
pocket again but she could feel the slow seep of blood
from the stinging slash of Fatima's assault.

Tense minutes passed. Bethany didn't know what to
do. Ahead of them the plain vanished into a rolling
landscape of dunes. Where on earth was Fatima taking
her? There was a sudden rustle of movement from the
front of the car. Bethany gasped as a veiled female shape

uncoiled from her hiding place on the floor and settled
herself into the front seat.

'Two women left the palace and two women will
return,' Fatima informed her smugly. 'Nobody will
suspect that you left in my company.'

'Where the heck are we?'

The Range Rover lurched to a halt in the shadow of
a great rolling dune. Springing out, the driver opened
the door beside Bethany.

'Get out!' Fatima planted both hands on her and gave
her a violent push.

Bethany got such a shock that she was easily unbal-
anced and went flying out headlong onto the ground. It
knocked the breath out of her lungs but didn't deprive
her of hearing Fatima's shrieked abuse and the prophecy
that the sun would wreck that pasty white skin of hers
and make her hair fall out so that no man would ever
want her again.

Bethany picked herself up and wrenched herself out
of the suffocating folds of the *chador*. 'You *can't* leave
me out here alone!'

As the Range Rover raked into reverse she very nar-
rowly missed being knocked flat by the swinging door
that Fatima had yet to pull shut. She leapt out of harm's
way and then stood there in the burning heat of the sun,
gripped by a brand of quite paralysing incredulity that
anyone could do such a thing. Then she was furious with
herself for trusting a woman who she had known was
blazing with jealousy and rage. She checked her watch
and paled. How many miles could that car have covered
in well over an hour? Worse, it would be dark soon.

Seeking a lookout point, she started climbing the
sliding wall of sand with raw determination. It took her
far longer and required far more effort than she had
expected. Near the top she bent double, struggling to
breathe in the hot air and overwhelmed by dizziness.
Finally achieving her objective, she strained her eyes

against the fiery blaze of the sun and thought that she was hallucinating when she saw the lines of black tents beginning less than thirty yards below her.

She blinked dazedly and looked again. Her terror of being found as a set of bleached bones after a long and painful decline brought on by thirst and third-degree sunburn died there and then. Indeed her attack of panic now made her feel distinctly foolish. It *was* a Bedouin encampment and a very large one. She did not believe in so miraculous a coincidence. It would seem that Fatima's driver might appear to do her bidding but he was *not* a maniac and he had chosen the drop site, aware that Bethany could come to little harm here. She started down the slope.

A clutch of colourfully clad children saw her first. They ran ahead of her, shouting at the top of their voices. Women peered out of dim tent interiors. Bethany followed the children until a whole horde of men piled out of an enormous tent and blocked her path, their dark, weather-beaten faces arranged in expressions that went from initial shock to outright rigid disapproval. They stood around her exchanging volleys of excitable Arabic and waving their hands about with gusto. Their reaction, so entirely foreign to the indelible rule of Arab hospitality, completely disconcerted Bethany.

A tubby little man with a grey beard, clad in gold-edged blue robes, paced forward and fixed stern black eyes on her. 'You are Prince Razul's bride?'

Red hair in Datar was like having two heads, Bethany decided. When some idiotic Englishwoman with a flaming head of hair came huffing and puffing out of the desert wastes wearing a silly, strained smile, evidently the locals could name her on sight. Zulema had not been exaggerating when she'd said that *everybody* knew about her. Now...should she say that she was *not* Razul's intended or should she play dumb?

'I am Razul's great-uncle, Sheikh Abdul al Rashidai Harun.'

Dumb wasn't likely to carry her through, she registered. Her smile slid away. She sensed the principles of family solidarity looming large, and she had the nasty suspicion that Sheikh Abdul found the sight of Razul's bride apparently loose and on the run in the wrong direction an offence of no mean order.

'I got lost,' she muttered stupidly, but she was so hot and so exhausted that the world around her was beginning to spin.

'You will not become lost again,' Sheikh Abdul announced, producing a mobile phone from his sleeve with a flourish. 'My nephew has a temper like a sandstorm, most dangerous when roused. It is a joy to behold.'

As Bethany swayed a woman tugged at her sleeve and she was carted off to the welcome shelter of a large tent. In daunting silence she was brought water to wash with, then was served with tea and a delicious selection of food. As darkness folded in the elaborate brass lamps attached to the tent-poles were lit. Left alone, she sank down on a kelim-covered ottoman and curved her cheek into a silk cushion, the vibrant colours of the gorgeous Shiraz rugs hung on the cloth walls of the tent swimming before her as her weighted eyelids sank down.

When Bethany finally awakened after a very restless night she was lying under a blanket which she immediately thrust off her, the stickiness of her skin telling her that a new day had begun. She shifted and sat up, her tumbled hair falling round her like a vibrant curtain of flame as she glanced at her watch. It was only eight. She lifted her fingers to thrust the tangle of curls off her damp brow and then she froze.

Sheathed in desert robes, Razul was standing mere feet away with the stillness of a graven image. Sizzling gold eyes as brilliant as sunlight in that hard-boned, hawkish face splintered into her with powerful effect. His complete silence was intimidating. But the most menacing thing of all for Bethany was the instant flood of pleasure and relief she experienced. That instinctive response was her worst nightmare come true.

She turned her head away. 'OK, so I made a break for freedom and ended up a long way from the airport,' she conceded in a tone of nervous irony. 'So what now? You bury me up to the throat in sand at the hottest part of the day, paint me with honey and set scorpions on me? Or do you just send me home in disgrace? What *is* the traditional approach?'

'According to tradition, I beat you.'

Bethany lost every scrap of colour, plunged into sudden, unavoidable recall of her aunt's disastrous marriage to an Arab. Violence had played its part in the final breakup of that union. 'That's something of a conversation-killer, Razul,' she murmured not quite steadily.

'*You left me.*' The intense condemnation with which he spoke mirrored the powerful anger that he was visibly struggling to contain.

'That's the problem with stealing women,' Bethany retorted with helpless defiance as her chin came up. 'The stupid creatures may well cherish a peculiar desire to regain their freedom.'

'Do you want me to lose my temper?' Fierce strain was etched on his startlingly handsome features.

And Bethany discovered that *yes*, she did. She *needed* a cure for the madness afflicting her, and the proof that he was the kind of male likely to employ his infinitely greater strength to the task of subjecting a woman would surely provide quite unparalleled therapy. She bent her head, her emotions in so much conflict that she felt torn apart. The madness of her own reasoning hit her hard. Had she enjoyed a single truly rational thought since she'd entered Datar? Angry bitterness consumed her in a sudden, scorching tide.

She slid upright, her jewel-bright eyes slicing back at him. 'Why not? Isn't this whole crazy mess your fault? It's certainly not mine! How dare you bring me to this country? And how dare you stand there now and try to intimidate me?'

'Do not raise your voice to me here where we may be overheard.' The pallor of his increasing anger had spread savagely across his high cheek-bones.

'I'll do whatever the hell I like. I don't belong to you like some sort of rug you can walk on when you feel like it, and you have no rights over me!' she blazed back.

'Have I not?' Razul bit out very softly.

'None whatsoever, so you can keep the macho-man act for your harem!' Bethany spat at him in a mood of pure vitriol, wanting every scornful word to find its target. 'Your chances of reducing me to the level of crawling round your feet are zero... I'd sooner slit my throat! How dare you talk about your *honour* when you've already got a wife? When I called you primitive, barbaric and uncivilised in England I was understating the case!'

His strong face a mask of fury, Razul moved forward with such terrifying abruptness that Bethany threw herself backwards over the ottoman and screamed. A powerful hand closed over her shoulder and began hauling her bodily back up onto the seat which she was endeavouring to employ as a defensive barrier. The sheer strength he exhibited sent her into even deeper panic, and another few strangled yells escaped her before Razul laid the palm of his hand firmly across her trembling mouth, enforcing her silence.

Huge green eyes, dark with fear, looked up at him as he pinned her flat.

'Keep quiet,' Razul intoned.

That controlled command wasn't at all what she had expected. As she braced herself for a blow, her shocked eyes grew even bigger. Her heart was pounding fit to burst behind her breastbone. The hard heat and weight of his body imprisoned her as securely as chains.

'My people will think I cannot control my woman but I know very well how to control my woman,' Razul asserted with savage quietness. 'In bed and out of bed. But I have never yet sunk to shameful violence, nor would I. Do you understand that, or is that beyond your understanding?'

In a daze of quivering uncertainty she stared back up at him and drowned helplessly in the entrapment of compelling golden eyes raw with anger and derision.

'So, *aziz*...one more scream and all you get is a bucket of water over you to douse your hysterics. Am I speaking English clearly enough for comprehension?'

Bethany gave a mesmerised nod under his hand.

With a final searing glance he released her.

She was still in a condition of such bemusement that she couldn't function. She had gone from rage to terror within seconds and lost control. A kind of appalled embarrassment was beginning to steal over her.

Razul stared down at her. 'You said...you said that I already had a wife. Was that some childishly inept attempt to further defame my character?'

She closed her eyes in sudden agony, assuming that he intended to lie to her. 'I *know* that Fatima is your wife.'

'I have never had a wife. I was betrothed at the age of twenty-two to Hiriz, my second cousin. Five years ago she died in a car accident shortly before we were to be married. Hiriz had a younger sister called Fatima,' Razul proffered in the same harsh, unemotional tone, although his biting tension was palpable. 'She is not my wife. Perhaps you would like me to call witnesses to this truth?'

Bethany slowly began to sit up. She was trying to remember what Zulema had said, and recalled that Fatima had at no stage claimed Razul as her husband but had

certainly looked pretty smug when Bethany had made
reference to what she had believed to be fact.

A quiver of darkly suppressed emotion rippled through
Razul's lean length as he studied her with icy dark eyes.
'Had you sought to know me at all, you would already
be aware that I do not believe in the practice of polygamy. Nor indeed does my father. One wife at a time
is quite sufficient for any man. But *no*!' Razul uttered
a harsh laugh. 'You do not see this. Your blind prejudice is shameful, your assumptions for an academic
mind inexcusable!'

White as snow and deeply shaken, Bethany made a
tiny, uncertain movement with one hand and then her
fingers dropped again. 'Razul, I—'

'In the name of Allah, an apology would be an even
grosser offence. No doubt you are still suffering from
the fantastic notion that my family harbour concubines
as well! We may be primitive, backward and painfully
unwesternised in our ways, but our standards of sexual
behaviour are far higher than those of your own society!'

Sinking ever deeper into a pool of stricken self-
examination while being engulfed by the greatest mortification she had ever been forced to endure, Bethany
could no longer meet that coldly condemning appraisal.

'After the death of Hiriz, young women were sent to
my father in the hope that I would choose a bride from
their ranks. While they were within our household they
were strictly chaperoned. They were also educated,
clothed and dowered at my family's expense . . . one very
practical reason why those daughters were offered by
their fathers. Until the spoils of oil wealth were shared,
many of them found it impossible to arrange suitable
marriages for their daughters. My relatives made matches
for them.'

'How could I have known that?' she whispered unsteadily.

'You did not want to know it,' Razul condemned. 'You preferred to believe the outrageous slander which appeared in newsprint. That article was a deeply offensive vilification which caused great distress to my family and to the families of the young women concerned. It was beneath our dignity to issue a denial of such salacious rubbish.'

Her head was spinning. He accused her of not having wanted to know the truth—a charge which pierced right to the heart of her turmoil, forcing her to see herself in a light which painfully exposed her every flaw. Her throat ached. It was as if he had held up a mirror and she wanted to shrink from her own reflection. Like most of her colleagues she had been willing to believe that newspaper article... why? It had provided them with a wonderful opportunity to pontificate on the outright hypocrisy of a society which demanded that young women live as cloistered ideals of perfect purity before marriage, while at the same time permitting the highest in the land to maintain concubines.

But Bethany had had the deepest motivation of all in choosing to accept that story as if it had been written in stone. Anything which she could use to reinforce the barriers she'd seen between herself and Razul had been welcome. It had been more grist to her mill of determined resistance, positive proof that he was every bit as alien in his way of life as it suited her to believe.

Suddenly Bethany, who had always prided herself on her seeking, *open* mind, was appalled by the unreasoning prejudice that she had unquestioningly chosen to harbour... simply because it suited her to do so. How much of that instinctive bias had she acquired in her teens when her mother's kid sister, Susan, had been going through the tortures of the damned in her ill-fated marriage to an Arab?

'I don't know what to say to you,' Bethany muttered unevenly.

He *wasn't* married. He had *never* been married. He had no other women in his life. Her brain was working in short, electrifying bursts, bringing down the barriers that she had hidden behind for years. Without that protection she felt frighteningly weak and vulnerable. Already she could sense a terrifying surge of relief longing for release inside her. Razul was free... and her last realistic line of defence was being smashed and put out of her reach. That scared the hell out of her!

'How did you injure yourself?'

Her lashes fluttered in bemusement as, without warning, Razul dropped down to her level and reached for her hand. The angry scratches which Fatima had inflicted stood out in stark contrast against her pale skin.

Her fingers quivered in his warm grasp. She looked down at him, watching the ebony crescents of his silky lashes drop near his cheek-bones, scanning the narrow blade of his nose, and her sensitive throat closed over altogether. When he wanted to be, he could be achingly gentle.

Gulping, she threw her head back, anguished guilt sliding like a knife into her heart. Did you really think that he was going to beat you up? she thought. Well, he knows now that you thought that too, and he can take it in his stride beautifully because you have taught him to expect nothing but misjudgement from your corner. She trembled, struggling to rein back the powerful emotions shuddering through her.

'Fatima did this,' he breathed.

'It doesn't matter,' she said chokily, not even caring how he knew that the brunette had been responsible for getting her out of the palace, or how he'd instantly divined who had inflicted those abrasions. Obviously he did know as he hadn't asked any questions.

'She threatened Zulema's family. Zulema had the presence of mind to approach me, but by the time she was able to see me the hour was late. I was with my father. These scratches need to be attended to in case infection should set in. They should have been dealt with last night,' Razul murmured, with a frown, releasing her fingers and straightening again.

She couldn't bear him to move away but she could feel the distance in him like a cold wall holding her at bay. And she didn't blame him—she really didn't blame him for his hostility. Green light...red stop-light. A hectic flush replaced her pallor. She remembered him saying that if he let her go she would regret it for the rest of her life. She remembered how outraged she had been when he'd told her that he was giving her a second chance.

Some truths were very tough on your pride, she acknowledged painfully. What a coward she had been two years ago, huddling blindly behind her prejudices, refusing to listen to her own intelligence except when it told her what she wanted to hear. The reality was that it had been easier for her to refuse him. She hadn't had the guts to cross over the barrier of her own insecurities. She had been afraid of the strength of that attraction, afraid of being hurt, and neither had been an unreasonable fear.

After all, there *was* no prospect of a future with Razul. To talk of marriage was insane. Of course, he hadn't been talking about a *real* marriage, she recalled—at least, not what she understood as a real marriage, though she had no doubt that he viewed this temporary contract business in quite a different light. Naturally his father, whose distrust and dislike of foreigners was well-known, didn't want one in the family on any other basis.

What she didn't understand was how to handle her own emotions. Why the hell hadn't she had an affair with him in England? She would have got this insanity out of her system then and been cured, she reflected resentfully. Within a very short space of time she would have realised that they didn't have a single thought in common, and her infatuation would have died a natural death. There would have been no complications, no agonies, no past to come back and haunt her now with regret and bitterness.

'I think we need to talk...' Bethany muttered uncertainly.

'I am always prepared to talk.' Disconcertingly, Razul's set mouth came very close to a smile.

Bethany swallowed hard, still so bewildered by her own emotional conflict that she was not at all sure that she ought to be saying anything to him. 'I have a...a suggestion to make.'

'Does it relate to your departure?' he breathed tautly.

'Yes...well, obviously it would be sensible for me to go home. But that...well, that doesn't mean that I...well, that I wouldn't be...' her skin burning, she stumbled helplessly over the words to verbalise her own thoughts '...open to the possibility of—well...er...not *here* in Datar, of course, but you can't be here all the time!'

Razul scanned her with unhidden fascination. 'I am lost.'

He wasn't the only one. Bethany had got cold feet. How could she possibly suggest to him that they had an affair? That sounded so cold-blooded, not to mention brazen, but on the other hand it was a considerably more realistic proposal than the idea of marriage in any form, she reminded herself staunchly.

'I am attracted to you,' she began again in a flat tone which concealed her embarrassment, 'and I am prepared to admit that I have not reacted in a very reasonable manner as regards that...er...situation. Had we explored that situation in a relationship two years ago...and again I admit that it was my fault that we didn't...but, had we done so, that would have been by far the most sensible solution—'

'To the problem of this attraction...excuse me...this situation,' Razul slotted in smoothly.

Relieved that he had so easily followed her reasoning, Bethany's gaze collided involuntarily with shimmering golden eyes and she snatched in a deep breath. 'Therefore it naturally follows that employing marriage as a resolution of the situation would be ridiculously excessive. This is not the nineteenth century, after all, and—'

'This is how I imagine you might speak in the lecture theatre,' Razul remarked.

A pin-dropping silence stretched.

Flames of angry pink burnished her fair skin. She decided to ignore that ungenerous comment. 'And we are both adults—'

'That is indeed a matter of opinion.'

'Look...will you stop interrupting me?' Bethany hissed at him in frustration. 'I am only trying to point out that, while I am not prepared to marry you, I am willing...well, open to the possibility of—'

'Exploring the situation in my bed?' Razul incised in a raw undertone.

Bethany turned scarlet. 'If you *must* put it that way...but I was thinking in terms of—'

'A cerebral affair?' he gritted.

'Well...' Bethany dropped her head, tied up in knots of horrible, mealy-mouthed discomfiture. He seemed to be going out of his way to make this more difficult for her. 'Whatever might conceivably develop...I haven't got a crystal ball—'

'Had you been blessed with one, you would have closed your mouth five minutes ago and kept it shut, but I thank you for your honesty!' There was a whitened edge to Razul's compressed lips now. 'I hope you are equally grateful for mine. My terms are marriage...marriage *or* you will be as one dead to me! I will never voluntarily rest my eyes on you again in this lifetime!'

Her jaw dropped. 'You can't be serious...'

'I have never been more serious,' Razul swore with savage bite.

Bethany was incredulous and furious into the bargain. She had laid her pride and her self-respect on the line. She had offered him a relationship which until today she had never once considered offering to *any* man. That had taken a great deal of courage, and even as she had voiced her proposition she had been frantically worried that she was impulsively overreacting to her own hopelessly confused emotions. 'Right now I could live with never seeing you again just fine!' she told him wrathfully.

Savage golden eyes raked over her. He spread his shapely hands wide and dropped them again with an air of cold finality. '*Inshallah*. Then I give you the freedom that you say you want. You may go. There is a helicopter out there. It will take you to the airport. There is a flight to London in two hours.'

Devastated by the assurance, Bethany gaped at him, her every expectation violently overthrown.

'You have half an hour to make your choice.'

'I don't need half an hour!' Bethany shot back at him, her eyes pure emerald in her hotly flushed face as she squared up to him. 'Five minutes would be too long!'

Razul slung her a slashing glance from molten gold eyes, every line of his lean, muscular length whip-taut. 'That is your decision, but be assured *aziz* . . . if you stay, you will be my wife by evening.'

'That is as likely as me taking flight without jet engines!' Bethany snapped in ringing disbelief. 'You have to be out of your mind!'

'We will see how out of my mind I am . . . *this* we will see.' He made it sound like a threat written in blood. His strong, hard features rigid, he swung soundlessly on his heel and swept out.

CHAPTER FIVE

NOTHING like choosing the magic words to speed the parting guest...'wife by evening'? Hah! thought Bethany. Razul was certifiably insane. She knew she would be into that helicopter so fast that she'd leave a trail of little flames dancing in her wake! Release...escape... freedom, here I come! Razul had decided to force the issue, which wasn't surprising, not when you took that mile-wide streak of mean, moody, macho conditioning and added it to all that ferocious pride. Well, she thought with murderous satisfaction, he had made a gross miscalculation. Her little Middle Eastern adventure had come to an end and very grateful she was too!

Her attention fell on the suitcase that she hadn't seen since her departure from the airport. She blinked, reading the message that went with its reappearance. Razul had clearly brought it with him. So, in other words, he had come prepared to face her with that choice. But *first* he had allowed her to make an outsize idiot of herself!

Her teeth gritting, Bethany was fired into sudden activity. She dug out her keys and unlocked the case. She had no plans to check in at Al Kabibi airport dressed in a caftan and silk slippers! Why the heck hadn't she noticed that suitcase sooner? For a few minutes there a tide of remorse had gripped her with temporary insanity. She had actually sunk low enough to offer herself on a plate. If only she had kept her stupid mouth shut she could have boarded that helicopter with every ounce of her dignity still intact!

She took her time getting dressed in a pair of light cotton trousers and a voluminous white T-shirt. Then she combed her hair and finally checked her watch. Fifteen minutes had gone. She walked the length of the tent, pushed aside the ornate hangings and looked outside. The blazing rays of the sun were glinting off the silver body of the helicopter parked in the centre of the camp. Perspiration broke out on her skin. She lifted her case.

You will never see him again.

She could handle that... of course she could; hadn't she got by for twenty-seven years without ever depending on a man?

Never is a long time.

Her teeth clenched. She thrust a furious hand through her tumbling hair. Damn him... damn him to hell and back! She was stronger than this. She was going to do the sensible thing no matter how blasted hard it was to do it!

All her life she had been prudent, practical and realistic. No nonsense, no silly romantic fantasies... well, only one, she conceded with boiling resentment. *Him*. Picking up her books on the library steps, smiling that soul-destroyingly charismatic smile, he had somehow stolen a part of her that she had never got back. Since then... always this nagging sense of loss, separateness, aloneness. She had hated him for having that power over her, and now she hated him ten times more as she wrestled with a hunger as frighteningly irrational as the unfamiliar sense of complete impotence now freezing her in her tracks.

Never is a long time...

What is the difference between an affair and a temporary marriage? an insidious little voice whispered. Stricken by the treacherous thought that had come at her out of nowhere, Bethany pressed unsteady hands to her hot face. She quelled that sly voice. Every fibre of her being revolted against being forced into a position that she had not freely and rationally chosen.

But where was her free choice when her only other option was *never* to see him again? And Razul would keep to that promise. Razul had the kind of dark, driven temperament which could make a sacred shrine out of self-denial. Overwhelmed by the emotional storm battling inside her, Bethany sank dizzily down on the edge of her suitcase. If thoughts had had the power to kill, Razul would have been dead. She was in mental torment. 'Never' stood like a giant wall between her and the freedom she cherished...

The rotor blades of the helicopter started up with a noisy, clattering whirl, and the tent walls rippled. Bethany, who made a virtue out of never crying, shocked herself by bursting into floods of furious tears. She despised herself; she hated him. In the space of forty-eight hours he had torn her inside out. He had cornered her and sprung a trap that she hadn't recognised until it was too late. Dear heaven, she would never forgive him for pushing her to the wall like this and forcing surrender on her!

'What is wrong, *sitt*?'

'*Everything*!' Bethany sobbed passionately before she focused on the speaker.

'Prince Razul was very angry. He was most disturbed for your safety. But on such a day his anger will melt away.'

Bethany's distraught gaze rested on Zulema's sympathetic face as the girl reached shyly for her left hand and clucked anxiously over the scratches. A sob still rattled in her throat as Zulema gently pressed her hand into a bowl of warm water from which the sharp odour of some form of antiseptic wafted. It stung like mad.

'I understand that your family was threatened by Fatima,' Bethany managed tautly.

'But I need no longer fear this threat.' Zulema smiled.
'Now my family live in Prince Razul's protection. He
will give my father new employment.'

'I'm glad.' Bethany drew in a shaky breath, drained
by her crying jag.

'I am glad our Prince does not marry the Princess
Fatima,' Zulema revealed in a rush of covert confidence. 'It is what the King wished but those who know
her well did not wish it.'

So Fatima had had the official stamp of royal approval. Razul had not mentioned that fact. No wonder
the brunette had been so bitterly hostile to Bethany's
arrival.

'What you saw in the courtyard...do not pity her.'
The younger woman looked surprisingly cynical. 'She
made a big scene to try and shame the Prince into sending
you away. It is wrong for a woman to embarrass a man
like that. If her father hears of it *she* will be sent away!
He would be disgraced.'

Zulema affixed a plaster to the scratches and then
stood up and clapped her tiny hands. Instantly her usual
two helpers appeared, laden with various articles. There
was a burst of voluble chatter from outside the tent.
Wrought-iron holders were set up and incense sticks lit,
their heavy perfume filling the hot, still air. An alu-
minium bathtub was marched past her and settled behind
the screen at the other end of the tent. Buckets of lightly
steaming water arrived one by one.

Bethany hovered in a daze of bewilderment until
Zulema drew her behind the screen. Very seriously the
little maid covered her eyes. 'I not look, *sitt*...only help.'

Bethany heard herself laugh, her fierce tension suddenly evaporating, and why not? Common sense insisted that Razul could not *possibly* be intending to really
go through with his threat to make her marry him. It
would be just too ridiculous. He had spoken in anger.
Later she would gently call his bluff and reason with

him, hopefully without offending that unquenchable
pride which was so much a part of him. It had been a
very melodramatic threat...but very Arabic and very
Razul, she reflected helplessly.

She would accept his hospitality for another few days
and see how she felt then. Really there was absolutely
no reason for her to go rushing off home like a Victorian
virgin threatened with ravishment! That would be a
repeat of the same cowardice that she had exhibited in
England. There was no good reason why, having come
this far, she should not allow herself the luxury of getting
to know Razul a little better. What would that cost her?
And, in the meantime, she could even begin her
research...

She slid into the warm, scented water, wryly accepting
Zulema's assistance and bending her head obediently as
her hair was carefully wetted and then shampooed.
Cocooned in towels, she emerged again and sat down to
have her hair combed out and her nails painted. Why
all the fuss? she wondered.

'You look tired, *sitt*. Lie down and rest for a while,'
Zulema urged. 'The party will last for hours.'

Party? So somebody was throwing a party. Her curiosity satisfied, Bethany smiled and lay down. She could
hear a helicopter.

When she opened her eyes again, she could still hear a
helicopter, or was it helicopters? She was surprised to
realise that she had slept for several hours but then she
hadn't had much sleep the night before.

Zulema extended a shimmering, heavily embroidered
golden caftan. It was really quite exquisite. The silk
flowed across her body with a wonderfully sensuous feel.
A vast square of gold chiffon was produced and draped
around her head. 'You look very beautiful, *sitt*,' Zulema
sighed admiringly. 'You come now?'

Bethany followed her out into the hot, still air. She only had to walk a few yards before she was in another tent the size of a marquee. It was crammed to capacity with richly dressed but mainly middle-aged and elderly women. One by one they came up to greet her and kiss her on each cheek. They were terribly friendly but nobody spoke English and Bethany was quite frustrated, for she would have loved to chat and ask questions. An enormous banquet was spread out on a white cloth in the centre.

Bethany wasn't very hungry but she picked at a few dishes out of politeness. The meal went on for ages but she wasn't bored. There was so much going on around her that she was fascinated, and when the food was cleared away the dancing started to the strains of Arabic music issuing from a huge set of speakers. It got very noisy, but everyone was having a good time and there was a lot of laughter, particularly when a very large woman took the floor to undulate and shake like a belly dancer.

'Please follow me, *sitt*.' Zulema appeared beside her out of the crush. 'It is time.'

As Bethany stood up the music went off. Time for what? she almost asked, but presumably Zulema meant that the party was now over, and she *still* didn't know what the celebrations had been about. There were loud cries of '*Lullah...lullah!*' She assumed these to be some form of goodbye angled at her, and she waved and smiled, which seemed to go down very well, before accompanying Zulema through the hangings at the far end which divided off a section of the tent.

Razul was standing there surrounded by older men. He looked so heartbreakingly handsome in a white linen robe with a dark blue, gold-edged overlay that her mouth went dry and her heart leapt like a dizzy teenager's inside her chest as she crossed the floor to him. A bearded old man was speaking and receiving the utmost solemn attention from his assembled audience.

When that same old man abruptly moved forward, reached for her hand and looped a scarf round her wrist, Bethany was astonished. He looped the other end of it round Razul's wrist and began speaking. Bethany froze. What the heck was going on? As her wrist was released again comprehension splintered through her in a violent wave and plunged her deep into shock. The old man had to be an imam or priest. Unless she was very much mistaken... but she *had* to be mistaken...

Her stricken gaze flew to Razul. A faint frown-line divided his ebony brows as he noted her pallor. Her eyes took a dazed flight over the grave-looking men on either side of them. Her teeth sank into the soft underside of her lower lip and the tang of her own blood tinged her tongue. A tide of dizziness ran over her, leaving her light-headed. Dear heaven, unless her intelligence was playing tricks on her, she had just taken part in a marriage ceremony in the role of...?

Bride? She, Bethany Morgan, who was as anti-marriage as a woman could possibly be, had just played an unwitting part in a ceremony to which she had offered no consent? Fathoms-deep in shock, she trembled. It couldn't be legal—it couldn't possibly be legal when she hadn't understood a word of it or even what was happening to her! The other men were filing out.

'What is the matter with you?' Razul murmured in a driven undertone.

Her hands clenched into fists. 'You ought to be locked up...' she told him in a quavering voice that sounded alien to her ears. 'I did not consent to marrying you.'

A dark rise of blood accentuated his hard cheek-bones. Stunned golden eyes flared at her. 'But I told you we would be married if you remained—'

'And did I say I *agreed*?' Bethany gasped, still seriously weakened by shock.

'You stayed...I took agreement to be given!' Razul returned in an equally incredulous undertone. '*Finally*, I believed, you had come to your senses!'

'There's a big difference between staying and getting married.' Bethany pressed damp palms to her cold face. 'Any sort of married,' she mumbled in faint addition, and then her anger stirred and she shot him an accusing look of pure outrage. 'You did it deliberately, didn't you? You knew I didn't believe that you were serious and you took advantage of my ignorance to—'

Without warning Razul closed hard fingers over her shoulder and forced her closer. 'Stop it,' he bit out. 'This is not the place for such a dispute...indeed, where could be the place for such a dispute? You are now my wife.'

His wife. Her stomach lurched. His wife...?

'Do not shame me before my family,' Razul warned, fiercely scanning her shocked eyes. 'For that I will never forgive and nor will they. These are serious proceedings...where is your respect?'

Every last scrap of colour drained from her cheeks. 'But I didn't know...I didn't realise—'

'Did I not tell you?'

'Well...yes, but I didn't *believe*,' she began shakily.

'Believe now,' Razul gritted.

'I don't want to,' she muttered in a very small voice, her lower limbs wobbling because the shock didn't recede, it only struck deeper as the minutes passed.

'Then why did you stay? Why did you not leave for the airport?' Razul demanded with a scorching undercurrent of embittered anger.

'I didn't think you were serious about *marrying* me...not today, here, now,' she whispered dazedly. 'And not in a ceremony like that.'

Had Razul really believed that by staying she was agreeing to marry him? Or had he relied on her lack of Arabic to carry her through to a point where only throwing the most appalling scene would have stopped the ceremony dead? By the time she had realised what was happening it had been too late. And why had she been so blind? When he had talked about marrying her she had not expected an actual *wedding*. A party and witnesses and the solemnity of an imam had not figured in her dim grasp of what such a temporary contract might entail.

'What was wrong with it?'

'Nothing... but I thought... you see, I thought,' she framed unevenly, 'that you were intending some sort of contract—'

'Contract?' he cut in with a frown.

'Fatima said—'

'What did Fatima say?' Razul prompted with sudden menace.

'Well, that you weren't planning on a *real* marriage, that it would be only a temporary arrangement.' Her voice began to join her lower limbs in the wobble effect as a flash of distinct incredulity darkened Razul's eloquent gaze. 'And, you see, I did once come across a written reference to this...er...this practice called *mut'a*.'

'*Mut'a*...' Razul whispered, and then he said it again, his flagrant distaste making Bethany wince. 'In Datar we do not recognise such arrangements for they are open to great abuse. Our rules of marriage are fixed by law and as legally binding as they are in your own country.'

'Oh,' Bethany mumbled.

'Had she told you I was a serial killer, would you have swallowed that as well?' When she failed to meet his fulminating gaze, Razul vented a derisive laugh. 'I am sorry to disappoint you, but we are really and truly married, and you have yet to give me a satisfactory response to the question of *why* you allowed that helicopter to go without you.'

Bethany worried tautly at her lower lip in the electric silence. Her mind was a complete blank.

'Why?' Razul repeated with awesomely unwelcome persistence.

'I plead a fit of temporary insanity!'

His strong features shuttered. Then as the murmur of voices sounded outside the tent his mouth twisted. 'You will feel even more married by the end of this day,' he forecast shortly as he drew back from her.

'And what's that supposed to mean?' Bethany asked shakily. 'I—' And her angry voice was choked off as an older man in a clerical collar came hurrying in, spluttering apologies for his tardiness and closely followed by an elegantly dressed woman and man.

'May I introduce you to the Reverend Mr Wilks, who is chaplain at the Royal City Hospital?' Razul drawled without any expression at all. 'My sister Laila and her husband, Ahmed, who have kindly agreed to act as our witnesses.'

Rooted to the spot, Bethany found herself shaking the minister's hand, receiving a warm embrace from the anxiously smiling older woman and another handshake from her husband.

'Blame Ahmed and me for the late arrival,' Laila told Bethany ruefully. 'We should have been here this morning but, as often happens in the medical world, the best laid plans can be wrecked by an emergency—'

'Your presence was required in the operating theatre and naturally we understand that the call to save human life takes precedence,' Razul interposed.

'But it has messed up things.' The attractive brunette sighed unhappily. 'I know you wanted the ceremonies the other way round and I was supposed to be here to make Bethany feel at home and introduce her to all the relatives, and instead she was left marooned at her own wedding reception... I'm afraid Zulema would *not* have been an acceptable interpreter in the eyes of the older generation. They are all roaring snobs—'

Ahmed moved forward, pressing a soothing hand to his wife's back. 'Do you not think that we should allow Mr Wilks the floor?' he murmured, with a twinkle in his brown eyes. 'You will learn, Bethany, that my wife rarely pauses for breath when she starts talking.'

Bethany summoned up a strained smile. She absolutely could not bring herself to look at Razul. He had intended the English ceremony to take place first, and if it had happened that way she would have known what was going on in time to stop it...but would she have? Would she have had the courage to call a halt in the presence of his family, to shatter the expectations of so many important people by refusing to marry Razul?

Dear heaven, it would have caused a riot, not to mention plunging him into a humiliation of immense proportions... No, she didn't believe that she would have had the nerve to do that to him when her conscience grudgingly suggested that she had played some part in the misunderstanding which had led to this ghastly conclusion.

'Shall we proceed?' the Reverend urged cheerfully.

When Razul had said that she would feel really and truly married by the end of the day, Bethany reflected in furious frustration, he had not been exaggerating. The service was the traditional one. She made her responses unsteadily, and when Razul grasped her hand to slide a wedding ring onto her finger she was as stiff as a clockwork doll. When she had to sign the register, her signature wavered. *Misunderstanding...?* Hell roast him, she thought in sudden, gathering rage; I'll kill him when I get him on his own!

'I am going to adore having another liberated woman in the family!' Laila laughed as the minister fell into conversation with Razul. 'I had to get married to gain my freedom, and our father is still recovering from the shock of seeing what he saw as my eccentric hobby become a career.'

'You're a surgeon?' Bethany questioned, struggling for some form of normal behaviour and finding it very hard.

'An obstetrician. Not much choice really.' Laila pulled a comical face. 'The Datari male is a macho creature but he would run a mile if he was faced with a female medic! But when he discovers there is a female doctor for his wife's most intimate needs he is delighted I exist and the women are too. I am very happy that you have become a part of our family, Bethany,' she said, with an embarrassingly sincere smile. 'And I am sorry that you have had to wait so long to—'

'It is time for us to leave,' Razul interrupted abruptly.

'Why are you in crown prince mode?' Laila asked, with a sudden frown.

'Laila—' Ahmed was flushed, clearly already well aware of the lack of bridal joy in the atmosphere.

Razul's sister subjected Bethany to an uncertain, questioning glance, her bewilderment and concern unconcealed. Bethany went scarlet with discomfiture.

'We will see you very soon. I hope you will be our first visitors,' Razul drawled very quietly.

They got one foot beyond the tent before Bethany heard a muffled surge of Arabic break from Razul's older sister. 'What is she saying?' she whispered helplessly.

'Forgive me if I choose not to translate.' His hard-boned features a mask of grim restraint, Razul headed for the waiting helicopter, leaving Bethany to follow in his imperious wake. Behind them the music broke out as the wedding celebrations started up again.

'Razul—?'

Screaming tension in every line of his lean length, he paused until she drew breathlessly level with him. 'You want to know what happens now? That is very simple,' he stated in a tone from which every drop of emotion had been ruthlessly erased. 'At the end of the summer

I divorce you. You go home. I take another wife. I will put this stupid, witless mistake behind me.'

'Take another wife'...? Bethany stared fixedly at the space where Razul had been. He was already swinging up into the seat beside the pilot. At a much slower pace she clambered into a rear seat where Zulema soon joined her. The rotor blades started up with a deafening whine, mercifully forbidding any further conversation.

CHAPTER SIX

BETHANY was in severe shock. One minute Razul told her that they were really and truly married, the next he dismissed their marriage as easily as if it meant nothing. In other words, it did mean nothing to him. It might just as well have been a temporary contract! Marriage had merely been the convenient device by which he'd intended to get her into his bed on *his* terms. Evidently she was to have been Razul's final fling before he settled down to the serious business of marrying someone suitable and acceptable, like Fatima, who came with gilt-edged fatherly approval. Musical wives like musical chairs.

Presumably they were now heading back to the palace... Well, he needn't think that he was going to lock her up there to moulder away until the end of the summer! Nor need he fondly imagine that when he descended from the Olympian heights of his outraged pride *she* figured on featuring on the entertainment list for his final fling. To put it equally bluntly, he had no hope!

The trip in the helicopter was short. Bethany alighted, her beautiful face set like pale marble. Only then did she realise that she was not where she had expected to be. She was surrounded by beautiful terraced gardens which were quite unfamiliar. Tamarisk and palm trees stood tall above lush slices of green grass and rioting tropical flowers. 'This isn't the palace...'

She turned but saw that Razul was still standing in the shadow of the helicopter. He was talking into a mobile phone, his intonation edged, his facial muscles clenched hard beneath his tawny skin. Whoever he was talking to, he did not appear to be enjoying the conversation.

Zulema answered her, 'The King's palace is only a short distance away, my lady. This palace is now the home of Prince Razul. It was where his mother lived. She died soon after the Prince was born. The King closed up this place, took his baby son and moved back to the old palace. It was very sad, for it is very beautiful, no?'

'No... I mean yes.' So Razul had grown up without a mother. Bethany crushed a tender green shoot of compassion in its tracks. What was that to her? she asked herself angrily, walking up a shallow flight of steps and beneath a carved stone entrance into a breathtakingly beautiful, marble-floored courtyard ringed by an arched cloister.

Dazzling panels of glazed tiles covered every wall. Water played softly in the silence, jetting down from a fountain set in the centre of a large pool. Beyond, yet another archway beckoned them into a magnificent hall the impressive width and length of a stretch of motorway.

Once in the hall, Bethany strolled through the nearest door into a large room, considerably surprised to find herself surrounded on all sides by antique furniture which would not have looked out of place in an English stately home.

'The Prince tells me that this is a drawing room,' Zulema informed her. 'We have lots of drawing rooms here.'

'Wonderful,' Bethany muttered rather weakly, and wandered across the width of the hall to walk into a highly traditional Arab reception room complete with sunken coffee hearth, heaps of cushions and the usual paucity of furniture. The same picture continued right down the length of that enormous hall—on one side, westernisation complete with elaborate furnishings and ornamental clutter, and, on the other, the simpler Islamic backdrop. It was peculiar, she reflected as she walked back outside again. Had the Western half been created for the purpose of entertaining foreign VIPs?

The sound of steps jerked her head round as she stood contemplating the fountain in the outer courtyard. Razul stilled several feet away, his suddenly screened dark eyes resting on her in much the same way as he might have regarded a grenade with the pin pulled out... very wary, coldly defensive, poised for a fight. And it disturbed her that she could tell exactly what he was feeling before he even opened his beautifully shaped mouth.

'Now you tell me why you did not leave when you had the opportunity,' Razul commanded.

Bethany's teeth gritted. 'Right now that is completely irrelevant.'

'Be warned that now you are my wife I will be less tolerant of your evasions.'

A shudder of raw resentment jolted through her. His wife... The unwelcome reminder was sufficient to send her temper rocketing again. Nor was she mollified by that stern intonation which implied that he was handing down a generous warning to a misbehaving child! She threw her vibrant head back, her emerald eyes flashing sudden fire. 'You run so true to type, Razul—'

'Explain yourself!' he breathed harshly.

Bethany loosed a laugh of scorn, thinking of how fast her aunt's adoring husband had changed his tune after their marriage. 'I'm well aware that the Arab male drops all charm and persuasion the minute he gets a wedding ring on a woman's finger. Then he feels secure. Then he feels he's free to be himself, master of his household and lord of all he surveys... and the much desired and courted bride becomes just one more possession to be used and abused according to his mood. Well, before you get totally carried away with that heady sense of being all-powerful, allow me to assure you that that ring on my finger means less than nothing to me!'

Razul stared back at her, and it was like standing in the centre of a swirling storm. Every poised line of his lean length was utterly still. And yet the fierce tension that emanated from him hit her in electric waves. His silence alone was a form of intimidation. Inside herself Bethany felt the compelling force of a temperament that was stronger by far than her own, and in immediate rejection of that disturbing suspicion she wrenched off the ring on her finger and sent it spinning into the pool. It vanished in one tiny splash.

The charged silence began to feel like a swamp that she was trying to wade through—heavy, unyielding...

'That ring is the symbol of a farce!' Bethany condemned, furious that she sounded defensive.

Razul was rigid and very pale. He appraised her with hard dark eyes as cold as a wintry night. 'Your manners are appalling and you have a temper as unruly as that of a spoilt child. You lash out blindly, careless of the insults you offer. I suspect this comes from a lifetime of regarding no counsel but your own, but you are foolish indeed if you believe that I will endure such displays. Retrieve that ring,' he ordered.

Furiously flushed and outraged by his censure, Bethany glared back at him, breathing fast. She was so mad that she wanted to jump up and down on the spot.

'Without it you will not enter my home,' Razul informed her grimly.

'Fine! I didn't want that stupid ring in the first place!' she slung back.

'No...you wanted me to treat you like a whore...but that hope could yet be fulfilled—'

'I beg your pardon?' Bethany gasped.

'With every offensive word and gesture you diminish my respect for you. I look at you and I ask myself, Was it for this woman that I have offended an honoured father?' Razul derided harshly. 'What should have been a day of joy has descended into a vale of tears, dissension and regret, and I have no patience left. Retrieve that ring or spend the night out here... Without it I will not recognise you as my wife!'

'And you think that matters to me?' Bethany blistered back shakily, her hands curling into fists.

'I believe that you should learn what it is like to be treated like a possession to be used and abused according to my mood. Only then, perhaps, will you appreciate that I have never treated you as a lesser being...until now.'

If he seriously thought for one moment that she was about to clamber into that wretched pool and get soaking wet, he had better think again fast! Bethany thought. She stood there like a stone statue as he swept off. She could see two guards standing just inside the door of the entrance into the palace; their presence was natural when Razul was within but, even so, rage engulfed her at the sight of them. She now had an audience. Her teeth ground together, murderous heat quivering through her. So he actually thought that he was going to teach her a lesson, did he?

How dared he stand there and tell her that she had appalling manners...how dared he? How dared he come over all superior and look down that arrogant nose at her with that aura of icy hauteur? Had she asked to be dragged out to Datar and married twice over? And if he had offended his father by marrying her was that *her* fault? The sun beat down on her unprotected head. She drew back into the shadows and finally dropped down onto her knees, which was damnably uncomfortable on that cold marble floor. I hate him...I hate him, she raged inwardly with real violence.

An hour passed painfully slowly. Who was the clever woman who hadn't got into the helicopter? Who was the clever woman who'd fondly imagined that she could reason with Razul...*control* him? Who had got up on her feminist soapbox and accused him of sins that he had not yet had time to commit . . . and who had put *this* blasted exercise in humiliation into his head in the first place?

She stood up again, stiff as a board, and tears of furious frustration scorched her eyes. Razul was the only person alive who could make her lose her temper to such an extent! Oh, to hell with it; she wasn't prepared to sit here all night and freeze and starve to make some stupid, childish point! And possibly throwing away the ring had been a little over the top, but what she had really been doing was letting him know that, when he had uttered those fatal words, 'I take another wife', as if wives were exchangeable commodities, she had experienced a powerful need to demonstrate that their marriage·meant nothing to her either.

Down on her knees, she slid a hand into the pool and delved. It wasn't very deep and the water was crystal-clear, but could she see that wretched ring with the sun reflecting off the surface? Then a particularly bright glitter caught her eye near the centre. Her mouth compressed into a mutinous line. She stretched perilously across the surface of the pool and lost her balance, one knee sliding over the edge into the water, swiftly followed by the other. In a tempest of fury she picked herself up again, soaked to the skin by the splash, snatched at the ring and climbed out. She stalked, dripping, into the palace, leaving a trail of tiny puddles in her wake.

He's dead, Bethany swore to herself. He may still be walking around but he is dead! If he wants war, he has got war.

He didn't know you didn't want to marry him, a little voice whispered. She crushed it but the voice was remorseless. You wrecked his wedding day, you embarrassed him with his sister and brother-in-law, you insulted him all over again.

Her nose wrinkled as the tickly sensation of tears threatened. All of a sudden Bethany felt that she was at her lowest ebb of all time. So why didn't you get into that helicopter? she asked herself desperately.

And the answer came back loud and clear—simple, straightforward and yet devastating to her pride. The threat of never seeing Razul again had paralysed her and wiped out her self-discipline. The same sort of uncontrollable attraction which had made such a mess of her mother's life, and threatened to do the same to her aunt's, had found another victim in her. Maybe that self-destructive streak ran in her genes like poison, for this time she hadn't had the strength to walk away from Razul... He had pulled her in too deep and too fast, drowning her in the desperate force of her own hunger.

And that was her own fault, she conceded miserably. To protect herself she had refused to allow men into her life, but that self-chosen isolation had not prepared her to deal with Razul. Yet the biggest enemy she had was not him, but what lay within herself.

He was the ultimate forbidden male, the epitome of her most secret fears: phenomenally handsome, just like her father, incredibly charming, just like her father, polished at making extravagant gestures, just like her father, highly successful with women, just like her father. A truly killing combination of the worst possible male attributes. So how could she possibly *want* a man like that? What was wrong with her that she could see all those things and still not be able to switch off this terrible, weak craving?

She stood shivering in a strange room with blind eyes while Zulema ran a bath somewhere close by. Shell-shocked by a sense of her self-betrayal, Bethany hovered while Zulema helped her out of the wet, clinging caftan. Like a sleepwalker she sank into a warm bath. Abstractedly she rubbed at her arm, feeling a slight ache above her wrist.

'You like something to eat now, my lady?'

Bethany emerged from her punishing self-absorption to find herself garbed in a diaphanous white silk nightdress. As she looked down at herself uncomfortably and noticed the way her pale skin gleamed through the whisper-fine fabric, a hectic flush lit her cheeks. 'No, thanks...'

'You should not be afraid, my lady,' Zulema whispered soothingly.

Bethany blinked. 'Afraid of what?'

'Of Prince Razul...'

'I've never been afraid of a man in my life!' But even as Bethany loosed a shaky laugh of scorn she knew that she was lying. Razul had already tied her up in terrifying emotional knots, and only his sheer, appalling persistence had forced her to acknowledge just how far out of control she was. She had actually been prepared to offer him an affair...on her terms, on her ground, at her speed...but that hadn't been enough for Razul. Razul wanted total, absolute surrender. *Never*! she swore to herself fiercely.

'When a man comes to his woman for the first time it is natural for her to feel a little nervous.' Zulema gave her a shy, teasing smile. 'But on this night many women will sigh with envy and dream of taking your place in the Prince's bed.'

Bethany stopped breathing altogether and sent an incredulous glance in Zulema's direction, but the little maid was already backing out of the room. Then she shook her head in mute disbelief and breathed again. Of course Razul wasn't *coming* to her! This was not going to be the average wedding night, but then Zulema was blissfully unaware of the circumstances of their marriage and of the current level of animosity between them.

Restively she lifted one of the books that she had brought with her to Datar—a nineteenth-century travelogue on the desert way of life. It contained some extravagant, even laughable errors, illustrating the writer's misinterpretation and ignorance of Arabic customs and superstitions. But had she been any less arrogant or any more fair in her response to Razul? Anxiously she hovered, suppressing the suspicion that she had always behaved in a downright unreasonable fashion with Razul—wanting him . . . and yet hating him for her own weakness . . .

When the door opened she spun round with a frown of surprise and saw him. A stifled hiss of shock escaped her and momentarily she was paralysed. His brilliant dark gaze crossed the room, closed in on her, and then wandered over her scantily clad figure with a kind of deeply appreciative intensity which filled her with a fiery mix of furious resentment and embarrassment. She snatched up the robe that Zulema had left across a nearby chair and held it in front of her like a defensive barrier.

'What do you want?' Bethany demanded shrilly.

Sudden, unexpected raw amusement flashed through Razul's tawny eyes as he strolled closer. With an indolent hand he removed the golden *iqual* and headcloth, baring his dark, luxuriant head of hair. 'You need to ask?' he murmured lazily.

'What do you think you're doing?'

'What do you think I am doing?' Razul turned the question back on her without hesitation.

He was undressing, but Bethany refused to believe the evidence of her own eyes. 'I thought this was my bedroom—'

'Tonight it is ours.' Razul framed the words softly.

'I am not sharing this room with you,' Bethany informed him flatly.

'You will.' He shifted with innate, fluid grace to survey her. 'You are my wife.'

'Technically speaking—'

'I am not technically minded.' He shrugged off the black, gold-edged cloak with complete calm.

The breath shortened in her throat. 'Morally—'

'And what could you possibly have to say on that subject?' Razul interrupted with sudden, slashing derision. 'Or do you forget that only this morning you offered me the freedom of your body without the commitment of marriage?'

Flames of hot pink burnished Bethany's cheeks. 'I was...confused this morning—'

'Correction...you were desperate, and allow me to tell you what would have happened if I had agreed. Once you were safely back in England you would have shut me out again and discovered a hundred reasons why we could not be together!'

'That's not true—'

'Your retreat stops here...now...tonight,' Razul spelt out with silken menace. 'And you made that decision for yourself when you chose not to go home. I told you I would marry you if you stayed, and I have no need to justify my presence here on my wedding night. You are my bride—'

'No...I want to get an annulment when I go home!'

'That is one fantasy destined to go unfulfilled. Think again,' Razul advised, with a blaze of anger in his magnificent eyes. 'Or think of me as your lover and not your husband... At this moment I do not care, but be assured that the games you play are at an end. Tonight you will lie in my arms and we will make love.'

Bethany trembled with furious disbelief. 'If you think that I would allow you to use me like that, you're in for a severe shock!'

Razul dealt her a look of shimmering intensity that burned up the distance that lay between them. 'I think it is not I who will be shocked.'

'You said that marrying me was a stupid, witless mistake!' she threw at him incredulously.

'A mistake I have to live with until the end of the summer, and if I have to live with it you will live with it too!' Razul informed her with compelling emphasis.

'That is a totally unreasonable attitude to take!' Bethany seethed back at him.

'I am not feeling reasonable. Why should I be? You are no longer deserving of any special consideration from me. In honour I married you, and how am I repaid?'

'I didn't *want* to marry you!' Bethany reminded him hotly.

'Then why in the name of Allah did you not get on that helicopter?' Razul raked back at her in an intimidating roar.

'I . . . I—'

'I knew that would silence you . . .' Razul slung her a sizzling glance of splintering derision. 'But do not think that I do not know the answer to that mystery. I *know* what was on your mind!'

Bethany had turned very pale. 'How could you possibly know?'

'I know your arrogance—'

'*My* arrogance?' she queried, scarcely believing that he could accuse her of such a fault.

'You thought you could make me play your game. You believed that you could have everything your own way. But what lay beyond that piece of self-deception?' Razul demanded with contempt. 'The truth that you would go to any lengths to avoid. Your desire for me is stronger than your pride, stronger than your prejudices and stronger than any hold you now have over me . . . because *I* would have let you go!'

As he forced that unwelcome truth on her her teeth clenched and she went white. It was as if that half-hour of decision time out in the desert had been a contest between them—a battle of wills in which he had triumphed, and he was not about to let her forget that.

'So do not seek to punish me for your vacillation, for I gave you your freedom and you turned your back on it,' Razul reminded her with savage impatience. Smouldering golden eyes whipped over her and his expressive mouth twisted. 'And why do you still cringe behind that garment? You look ridiculous! I am not so stupid that I imagined a woman of your age and background would still be a shy virgin!'

'I think you're very stupid,' Bethany hissed, flushed scarlet by outrage and chagrin, but she was not about to drop that robe and stand revealed in an almost transparent nightdress, no matter how ridiculous he thought she looked!

'In that you are probably right.' A tide of fierce emotion clenched his startlingly handsome features. 'I should have been true to my own ideals. I should not have sought to make allowances for your less principled society. I had to overcome certain cultural reservations before I could ask you to become my wife, knowing that I would *not* be your first lover—'

'Did you indeed?' Bethany quivered on another energising gust of rage. Yet she received a grim satisfaction from the realisation that he was unaware of her inexperience. 'And how did you know that?'

His sensual mouth compressed. 'I am well aware that you shared your apartment with a man the year before we met. I learned that in England.'

Danny, one of her colleagues, temporarily finding himself without a roof over his head, had begged for her spare room, and she had acquiesced purely and simply because he was the only male friend that she had ever had . . . and he was gay. 'But Danny—'

'I do not wish to hear about that other man.' Razul dealt her a furious glance of reproach, his tension palpable. 'And had you not roused such bitter hostility within me today such unjust feelings would not have occurred to me, nor would I have referred to them.'

'But I'm so glad that you did! I can quite understand your reservations,' Bethany responded acidly, seeing the weapon that he had put within her reach and ready to use it if it held him at bay.

'I am not a hypocrite. I would not demand from you a standard which I cannot claim for myself. And, in the temper you have put me in, it is probably fortunate that you are not untouched,' Razul told her with controlled savagery as he impatiently began to unbutton his shirt.

A golden wedge of muscular chest sprinkled with curling black hair appeared between the parted edges of the shirt. Bethany turned away, her heart suddenly thumping madly inside her chest, her colour high as she dug her arms into the robe he had derided. 'If you're staying here,' she informed him in a voice empty of all expression, deliberately chosen to deflate any expectations that he might have, 'I shall be sleeping elsewhere.'

Without warning a pair of powerful arms closed round her from behind. 'No.'

'Please remove your hands from me.'

'No.'

'Razul—'

'I am done with being a gentleman,' he asserted, hauling her back into the hard heat of his tall, powerful body.

'If you don't let me go I will walk out of here to-morrow,' Bethany swore shakily, hot tears suddenly lashing her strained eyes as the evocative scent of him washed over her, but with every ounce of her remaining self-discipline she struggled not to surrender to her own weakness. 'And when I get home again I swear I will talk to the Press!'

In response to the worst threat that she could think of making, Razul went satisfyingly rigid. 'You would not do that—'

'I would!' she lied frantically, her throat closing over. 'And why not? Didn't you say you were prepared for a diplomatic incident? Well, I'll give you one!'

Razul slid his hands down to her hips and snatched her off her feet in one dauntingly strong movement. 'Then tomorrow you go nowhere!' He headed for the door and wrenched it open before she could even catch her breath. 'Nor any other day!'

'What the heck are you doing?' Bethany gasped, thoroughly disconcerted by the tempest of fury that she had unleashed.

He strode off down the dark corridor.

'Razul...put me down!' Bethany ordered.

He kept a tight grip on her as he took a set of stairs at speed.

'Razul—'

'Close your mouth!'

'I'll scream!'

'Why not? In every tight corner you scream. Other people talk, you scream.'

'I just don't want to get any more involved with you...can't you understand that?' Bethany suddenly demanded in a voice an octave higher. 'I don't want to be married...I don't want an affair either! I just wish I had never met you!'

'Coward,' Razul jeered, thrusting wide some sort of a door with holes in it.

There was a metallic clang as it swung shut. 'How dare you call me a coward?'

'You have a streak of yellow down your backbone so wide I could find you in the dark!' Razul flashed back.

'It's not cowardice, it's common sense!' Bethany retaliated in outrage.

'And your cowardice took you all the way to Canada the last time...but not this time,' Razul informed her from between clenched teeth. 'As my wife you will have as much freedom as a criminal on parole, and you can thank my father for that. He never recovered from the humiliation of my mother's desertion. The female members of my family are the only women in Datar who cannot leave the country without a visa signed in triplicate by their husbands or fathers! To think that I should live to be grateful for such a medieval law!'

His mother's desertion? His mother had walked out on his father? Before she died? Well, obviously before she died, a dry little voice pointed out. Bethany cleared her swimming head of the irrelevancy. 'Put me down!' she demanded again.

Astonishingly he did so, only for it to become clear that that had been his intention in any case, for, a split second later, lights illuminated their surroundings. Bethany stole a dazed glance over the exotic splendour of the vast room they stood in. A simply huge bed hung with elaborate hangings stood in state on a marble dais. Her attention wandered over to the vibrant colours of the swirling murals.

She tilted her head, the better to interpret those pictures, and then flags of scarlet burned her cheeks. The act of love between a man and a woman was depicted in a series of graphic but highly artistic illustrations which she was severely embarrassed to look at in Razul's presence.

'For an anthropologist you are astonishingly prudish.' Razul surveyed her as though he had just learnt something fascinating about her.

'Where are we?' she enquired uncomfortably.

'My harem...did I not promise to bring you here?' Razul sliced back softly. 'Truly I honour you, for no European has ever seen these rooms.'

'And exactly why have you brought me down here?' Bethany snapped, infuriated by her inability to foresee what Razul might do next.

'Until you faithfully promise me that you will remain until the end of the summer, I will keep you here.'

Bethany turned to fix shattered green eyes on him, and any desire to ask him if he was serious was quashed by the unyielding set of his strong features. She swallowed hard and staunchly reminded herself that this had not been one of the most ego-boosting days of Razul's gilded royal existence, and, on those grounds, she was generously prepared to make certain allowances for his temper. 'That is a quite barbaric concept but I am convinced—'

'But surely only what you would expect from me?' Razul cut in grimly. 'As this day dawned you called me a barbarian and it is true that you unleash that side of my nature.'

'Only in the middle of an argument,' Bethany protested breathlessly.

'No...in argument with you I have subdued my natural instincts,' Razul told her, with a harsh laugh. 'I have quelled my temper, bitten my tongue and restrained my passion on your behalf. In an effort to gain your trust I have withstood the most base insults ever offered to me and I have forgiven you over and over again. I have also tolerated screams, tantrums and an attack of cold feet which would have driven most men to commit murder! But I tell you now that I will do it no more...my generosity is at an end.'

That sounded incredibly threatening. With difficulty, her colour high, Bethany cleared her throat in the claustrophobic silence. 'And what is that supposed to mean?'

'I will not lie down to be walked on by any woman!' Razul spat out at her with ringing bitterness. 'So, if that is what it takes for a liberated woman to accept a man, you will never find me acceptable!'

'I wasn't aware that I was—' she began in bewilderment.

'From now on I will be true to my own instincts,' he interrupted. Fierce emotion had clenched his facial muscles taut. 'I was conceived in the heat of the desert sun and I was born a true son of the sands, for I have nothing of my mother in me. No ice runs in my veins, no cool calculation controls my need for you. I know what I want. I know what I feel. I want to lock you up and hold you in purdah as my forefathers kept their women for their eyes alone. You *make* me feel like that!'

Glittering golden eyes scorched into hers with such ferocious intensity that she took a clumsy step backwards. 'Less than fifty years ago we would not have had this problem. I would have claimed you and taken you to my bed the same day I first saw you. I would have suppressed your rights with immeasurable pleasure! You would have known then that you belonged to me heart and soul. You would have been *honoured* to bear my ring on your finger—'

'You wouldn't have lived long enough to put it there!' Bethany asserted in a shattered rush of defiance, her emerald-green eyes spitting sudden fire.

'No?'

'No!'

Razul unleashed a slow, burning smile of sheer sensual threat and strolled fluidly closer. 'Then prove to me that you are not a coward. Prove to me that the same desire that flames in me does not flame in you... Come here, lie in my arms...reject me then,' he challenged.

'No bloody way!' Bethany gasped with heartfelt sincerity.

'Chicken,' Razul derided softly, stalking her across the depth of the room with the innate expertise of a natural predator.

CHAPTER SEVEN

'STAY away from me!' Bethany shrieked as she found herself backed up against the bed.

Razul stilled six feet from her and began to remove his clothing with slow, measured cool. 'You will not say that to me again. It is yourself that you fear, not me. Surrender may injure your pride but you will gain from the experience. A woman who denies her own womanhood is not complete—'

'I've never heard so much rubbish in my life!' Bethany watched his clothes dropping to the floor with her heart in her mouth and an unfamiliar clenched sensation gripping her stomach. She shivered violently. 'Don't you dare come near me!'

'Truly it takes a man among men to face such a wedding night.' Razul threw aside his shirt with an alarming air of purpose. 'But you will find that I am equal to the challenge,' he swore. 'And I have not descended to the intolerable humiliation of doing women's work to ingratiate myself into your bed as my predecessor did!'

'Excuse me?' Bethany mumbled dazedly, only half her mind functioning, as a superb golden torso straight out of her most embarrassing and secret fantasies emerged in reality. Her helplessly mesmerised gaze locked onto broad shoulders, powerful pectoral muscles and the pelt of black hair hazing his broad chest which dipped down over a flat, taut stomach into a silky furrow...and? Looking away was the hardest thing she'd ever done.

'That grovelling excuse for a man you allowed into your home and bed three years ago!' Razul gritted with a flash of white teeth. 'I heard the jokes about him. Your housewife, they called him, and laughed about how he cleaned your apartment and cooked your food and waited on you hand and foot...'

For a split second Bethany focused on what he was talking about. Danny's cooking had been out of this world, but his constant need to tidy up around her had in the end driven her batty because she had begun to feel like a lodger in her own home. Evidently Razul had missed out entirely on the one fact that had made Danny an acceptable temporary guest... his sexual orientation.

'But that...that...' She made the mistake of looking back at Razul, and what she had been going to say went clean out of her head again. Her startled gaze fell on narrow hips, long, lean, darkly haired thighs, and the shockingly visible thrust of male arousal displayed by the black briefs which he was in the very act of removing. Bethany froze and closed her eyes but somehow just a fraction too late, her innate shyness suddenly coming into unexpected conflict with a lowering surge of positively adolescent curiosity, which was duly punished. Dear heaven, she reflected dazedly, planting a hand to steady herself on the edge of the bed as her legs gave way, were all men *that*...?

'I will not emasculate myself to curry favour with you,' Razul informed her with wrathful intensity. 'But I will give you pleasure such as you have never known before in that bed, and we will see then which you prefer...man or wimp.'

Wimp, she decided helplessly, deeply shaken by her first view of a rampantly aroused male, and yet, on another level, quite beyond her comprehension, she felt all hot and sort of quivery deep down inside. Her fingers clenched convulsively into the bedspread beneath her as she fought for a window of reason in the blankness of her mind.

'I realise you're angry with me...'

'Release in the wondrous glory of your body will dispel all anger,' Razul said thickly, suddenly right there in front of her, determined hands peeling the robe from her shoulders, trailing it off and tossing it aside before she even knew what he was doing. 'And be assured that when the dawn breaks you will still be in my arms, as befits my bride.'

Before she could even part her lips, Razul gathered her up into his strong arms, but he threw back the bed-spread and laid her down in that bed with surprising gentleness. Instantly she crossed her arms over her breasts, horribly self-conscious about the scanty nature of her attire. As Razul gazed down at her from beneath dense black lashes that were longer than her own her heartbeat went haywire, her breath catching in her throat. Absolutely overpowered by that molten gold appraisal, she lay there, held strangely still and captive by a feeling much more powerful than any she had ever experienced.

A slight frown-line drew his winged brows together. He stroked a forefinger mockingly over the back of one of her hands. 'Why do you seek to hide yourself from me?'

Bethany lowered her eyelids. It took an enormous effort of will to close him out but it helped, it really did help, to get her brain back again. Her teeth ground together as she became even more rigid. 'I don't want this...'

'Have I frightened you?'

'Of course not...I am just trying to be the voice of reason here!' she gasped, whipped on the raw by the suggestion.

'Close your mouth again,' Razul suggested very gently. 'But open your eyes...'

That could well be fatal. It terrified her that he might know that too...that when she looked at him she had the resistance of a sex-starved teeny-bopper, and that the simple knowledge that he was lying beside her without a stitch of clothing on was quite sufficient to reduce her normal composure to the consistency of jelly. 'Don't take this any further,' she advised shakily.

'What did this man do to you?' Razul demanded with sudden, growling ferocity.

Involuntarily her lashes flew up in astonishment, trapping her into searing contact with his blazing gold eyes.

'You are terrified... If this man has hurt you I will seek him out and kill him with my bare hands!' Razul seethed with naked violence.

'I am not terrified,' Bethany protested, her pride stung. 'I am simply trying to prevent you from doing something we will both regret!'

Razul leant over her like a tiger about to spring, black fury engraved on his strong features. 'What did this man do to you?' he demanded again.

'Nothing, you bloody idiot!' Bethany screeched back at him, losing all patience. 'He was gay!'

Razul stilled, his ebony lashes dropping low. 'Gay?' he whispered in a dazed tone.

'Right... Now that we have that complication out of the way, is it possible that you could think of the ramifications of consummating this ridiculous marriage?'

'Gay...' Razul said again.

'A man who does not feel attracted to women,' Bethany supplied bitingly in her desperation.

With a deeply disturbing air of relaxation Razul settled fluidly back down on his side and propped his chin on the heel of one shapely hand to survey her furiously flushed face and her still tightly crossed arms. The compressed line of his mouth abruptly slashed into a shimmering smile of unholy brilliance. 'Truly I am a bloody idiot...'

'What are you smirking at?' Bethany hissed as she began to sit up.

A strong hand reached out and met her shoulder to press her inexorably back down again. 'Would you like me to switch the lights out? Would you feel less shy?' Razul murmured wickedly.

Her teeth clenched. 'I am not shy! I am merely attempting to save us both from a dreadful mistake...if you would only listen to me.'

'I listen...' He smiled again.

That smile literally clutched her with icy fingers of dread...it made her heart pound insanely. 'We have both agreed that this marriage was a mistake...right?'

'Wrong—'

'And in the light of that mutual agreement... What do you mean *wrong*?' Bethany grasped his word belatedly, her voice petering out to an unsteady halt.

Huge green eyes were entrapped by scorching gold ones. She stopped breathing, and without warning every inch of her taut body was poised on the edge of a sensual anticipation so intense that it made her head swim.

Razul murmured something in Arabic and slowly lowered his dark head, brushing his mouth softly across the tremulous curve of hers. She quivered violently as he let the tip of his tongue intrude between her lips, and she could feel the desperate force of her own craving threatening to break through and sweep away all rational thought. It petrified her. She lifted a hand and pressed it against his shoulder, felt the heat of his satin-smooth skin at the same time as he gathered her close, spearing his fingers into the tumbled fall of her vibrant hair.

Her heartbeat hit another terrifying peak as the heat of him enfolded her and the pressure of his firm mouth became inexorably more insistent. He employed his tongue in a glancing foray deep into the tender interior that she would have denied him, and her muscles jerked, a burst of shuddering pleasure catching her up in its tormenting grasp and making every sense scream with sudden frustration.

Her hands sank into the glossy thickness of his hair, holding him to her as the pulsebeat of desire thrummed her every tensed muscle. What are you doing? a voice shrieked somewhere in the depths of her blitzed brain, but she was powerless against that voice as the dam wall of her own resistance cracked, unleashing all the hunger that she had suppressed for so long. An incoherent moan sounded low in her throat as he turned up the heat in that ruthless kiss and with erotic mastery emulated a far more intimate possession. Her temperature rocketed, driven sky-high. Hot, drowning pleasure gripped her.

'Razul...' she mumbled thickly as he released her reddened mouth.

With a shimmering smile he brought her hands down from his hair and pressed his lips gently to the centre of each palm. Her dazed eyes clung to his as he brushed the narrow straps of silk from her taut shoulders, and she made a sudden movement of panic as reality threatened to break through the spell that he had cast over her.

But he crushed her mouth under his again and the hunger came back in a blinding wave that drove all before it. When she surfaced, like a novice swimmer who had dived too deep, her breasts were bare, rising full and swollen with shamelessly engorged pink nipples. Razul closed a restraining hand over hers as she attempted to cover herself from his heated appraisal.

'Do not be ashamed... rejoice in your beauty as I do,' he urged huskily. 'Your hair holds the glory of the dawn and your skin the pristine glow of a white camellia.'

As she lay there, feeling her whole body strain towards him, her breath caught in her throat.

'Pure... without flaw.' Razul curved reverent fingers to one quivering mound, and her stomach clenched and her teeth gritted, her eyes closing on the bite of intolerable sensation as his thumb rubbed across an achingly sensitive nipple.

He cupped her breasts, shaped them, explored them with expert hands and then dropped his dark head to engulf a straining pink bud in the heat of his mouth, letting her feel the graze of his teeth and the sensual stroke of his tongue. Her heart hammered, all control torn from her as her back arched, a fevered moan wrenched from her as a current of electric excitement coursed through her. All of a sudden she was burning alive on a rack of tormenting pleasure and sinking ever deeper into its thrall.

She couldn't stay still. Her nails dug into the smooth sheet beneath her and then fluttered instinctively up to him, biting into his shoulders, snaking up into his hair, until, with a stifled groan, he took her mouth again with a passionate urgency that consumed her, a strong thigh sliding between hers as his fingers splayed across the quivering muscles of her stomach.

He bent his head to her breasts again, covering her already fevered flesh with hot, hungry kisses. He moved and wrenched at the silk barrier wrapped round her slender hips, smoothing a caressing hand along the silken stretch of one thigh, tracing the length of that trembling limb to the tangle of fiery curls which shielded the very heart of her. A shocked sound parted her lips as he found the source of the most unbearable ache of all.

He leant over her, one hand clenched in her tumbled hair as her head moved restively back and forth on the pillow. Her eyes flew wide, glazed with passion. He looked down at her like a lithe dark conqueror, his glittering golden eyes locking with hers as he pressed his knuckles skilfully to the most agonisingly sensitive spot in her entire thrumming body and murmured roughly, 'Now tell me that you did not imagine this the very first time you laid eyes on me. Tell me that you did not see yourself lying under me, your body on fire for my possession ...'

A kind of appalled awareness flooded Bethany,
memory dragging her back two years in the blink of an
eyelid. She remembered time stopping dead as he'd
walked towards her, devouring her with that burning gaze
as if she were already *his*, as if he only had to look to
possess, as if all her life she had been waiting for that
one moment...and for *him*. And she had had a vision—
an instantaneous, utterly wanton vision—of him
throwing her down on a bed in the heat of passion and
forcing her with every erotic inducement in his reper-
toire to surrender to his sexual dominance. That image
had been so shattering, so intense and so utterly terrifying that it had taken her an entire twenty-four hours
to recover from the encounter.

'I...I—' she gasped.

'One look and you wanted me—'

'No!'

'Instantly, desperately, unforgettably,' Razul gritted,
scorching her with his savage golden gaze. 'You felt what
you had never felt before. A sexual recognition so
powerful, so consuming that we both saw the same
thing—'

Her lashes fluttered on suddenly wild and furious eyes.
'No—'

He moved an expert hand, like a torturer bent on in-
terrogation, and she cried out loud, unable to stifle that
helpless moan of intolerable pleasure or to prevent the
immediate jerk of her unbearably responsive body.
'Admit it,' he intoned with a feral flash of white teeth
and the kind of awesome tenacity which terrified her.

'You bastard!' she sobbed in an explosion of frustration and emotional stress. 'All right...all
right...yes...yes...*yes!*'

Having triumphed, Razul dealt her a sizzling smile in
reward for her surrender and lowered his lean, hard
length to hers again. He pressed his mouth hotly to the

tiny pulse flickering madly above her collar-bone. 'You are my woman—'

'No—' she panted in despair.

'And if I had lifted you up and kissed you breathless instead of trying to communicate in my very poor English you would have fallen at my feet—'

'*No!*' she moaned in anguish, furious with him—so furious that she was on the brink of explosion but she couldn't harness that energy into attack, couldn't control the shivering, tormented reaction of her body and the clawing need that he had mercilessly kept at boiling point.

'Yes.' With a husky laugh he ran the tip of his tongue down the valley between her heaving breasts then smoothly changed direction to encircle the engorged peaks that he had already caressed to throbbing sensitivity. He made her gasp and writhe while he sent his fingers travelling teasingly along the smooth stretch of one inner thigh, charting every tiny clenching muscle and following them to the very heart of her.

Her hips jerked wildly under the onslaught of that exploring hand. It felt as if every atom of her fevered being was centred there, and every caress drove her a little bit crazier until she was clutching frantically at him, finding his provocative mouth again for herself, desperate for any contact she could get, desperate for the agony of hunger attacking her to be assuaged.

'I will try not to hurt you,' Razul murmured raggedly. 'But you are very tight and it has been so long for me...'

He had driven her to such a pitch of excitement that she was completely out of control. Nothing mattered, nothing impinged on her fevered state but the devouring need for that intolerably aching emptiness to be filled. He slid between her parted thighs and raised her up to him with strong hands, and the hot, hard surge of his manhood thrust against her softness. She gasped and stiffened, lashes flying up on fearful eyes.

'Don't tense,' he grated rawly as he sought an entry to the moist welcome he had prepared for himself.

'Please...' And she meant to say 'don't', but her lips wouldn't form the word. She was so excited, so unbearably aroused that the first thrust of his slow invasion wiped out her ability to talk or think.

He arched lithely over her, the hair on his chest abrading her taut nipples, and ravished her mouth before he plunged home into the very heart of her, and the sharp pain froze her in shocked rejection. As she cried out he released her lips and stared down at her, his golden features clenched by the strain of the control that he was imposing on his own fierce desire, but his eyes were as vibrant as flames as they swept over her with possessive pride. 'Now you are truly mine, *aziz*,' he intoned with savage satisfaction.

On the outer edge of pain she was sucked back down into a well of hot sexual excitement. The feel of him inside her, stretching her, filling her, was so intolerably intimate and pleasurable that she whimpered deep in her throat. In reaction he shifted again, penetrating deep with a groan of answering hunger. And then the last scrap of self-awareness fell away from her as he began to move in her, possessing her with long, powerful strokes that enforced his dominance and her surrender.

She was overwhelmed by her own shattering response, caught up in his stormy rhythm, her breathing fractured, her pulses rising to screaming pitch as her heart slammed against her ribcage with his every fluid movement.

The primal drive to satisfaction took over, making every skin-cell sing as he drove her to a frenzied climax of savage passion. Her body jerked like a rag doll's as the explosion of heat started deep down inside her and then splintered through all of her, devastating her, blinding her, deafening her, leaving her stunned by sheer pleasure. And, as she wrapped her arms tightly, instinctively round him and clung through the quivering aftershocks, the most shattering truth of all came to her while all her defences were down... You love him; you've always loved him.

It was like falling into a great black hole without warning. Reality hit Bethany hard. Nothing had ever shaken her as deeply as that head-on collision with the seething emotions that she had fought and denied to the last ditch.

She loved him but she had repeatedly assured herself that she was only suffering from a foolish infatuation, but foolish infatuations did not last this length of time nor cause such continual pain and conflict. Razul was everything she shouldn't want in a man when she had never wanted a man in the first place. She should have hated him on sight! And she had tried to hate him—oh, yes, she had tried—but she had failed so completely that she had refused to face her own failure.

She was still fathoms-deep in shock as Razul rolled over onto a cool spot in the vast bed, carrying her indolently with him. In the thick silence, imprisoned in the circle of his arms, she listened to the soft rasp of his breathing and the still accelerated thump of his heart and trembled, convinced that if she tried to get up her legs would fold under her, equally convinced that if she made a single evasive move he would haul her back to him like a rebellious child, because now she knew and he knew who was *really* in control... and that reality was like a hot iron searing her sensitive flesh. Love had got inside her and made a nonsense of her efforts to protect herself.

But how could she have known that he would use that wanton sexual hunger of hers as a weapon against her? She *should* have known, she told herself painfully as she recalled the controlled dark fury and outrage which her rejection of her wedding ring had provoked. Razul had decided to put her in her place and, lo and behold...and

this was not a surprise... her place was flat on her back
in his bed. And she saw now that there had been absolutely no way that Razul would have allowed her to
sleep alone, not after the way she had behaved, not when
this had been what he had wanted from her all along.

Her eyes stung fiercely. For the first time in her adult
life she felt weak and inadequate. She had never needed
anybody since childhood, had never allowed herself to
need anybody, but Razul had *made* her need him. He
had got beneath her skin and blown her every defence
sky-high.

'Forgive me for hurting you,' Razul sighed.

Her teeth ground together as she recalled his primal
satisfaction at that instant of sexual possession. She attempted to shift out of the incredible intimacy of his
embrace. His arms tightened. Her eyes flashed and she
lifted her head. 'You enjoyed it,' she condemned.

He tautened, paled and dealt her a look of such sudden
flashing fury that her stomach turned over. 'I did not
enjoy hurting you,' he countered in fierce rebuttal. 'But
I took natural pleasure and pride in your purity. I have
never lain with a virgin before. I did not expect to find
you innocent, and that you should give me such a gift
on our wedding night meant a great deal to me. I will
not apologise for that.'

'I wish I'd slept with a hundred men!' Bethany
snapped, her colour high.

'But you didn't,' Razul murmured with a slumbrous
satisfaction that he did not even bother to try and
conceal. 'You waited for me.'

'I did not wait for you!' she blazed.

'The question is academic now. Why, after the joy we
have shared, are you again attempting to fight with me?'
he enquired almost teasingly.

He was so gorgeous. Black hair, golden skin, stunning
eyes and a mouth as wicked as it was innately sensual.
Suddenly it hurt to look at him and feel the instant leap

of her own possessive pleasure in him. She was in torment, emotions surging tempestuously inside her. Love at first sight. She had never believed in it and yet it had happened to her. She had fallen head over heels in love with him the first time she'd seen him and she should have known it—she should have known it long ago!

She had been in agony for him at that college dinner when he hadn't been sure of what cutlery to use, and at each course he had watched her covertly and she had made something of a show of picking up the right utensils purely for his benefit. And when she had found it quite impossible to shoot him down in flames until the bitter end, because she was so painfully conscious of that fierce pride of his, she should have known *then* that Prince Razul al Rashidai Harun had a hold on her far stronger than any infatuation.

She could have wept now for her own blind stupidity. Had she acknowledged her own feelings, she was bitterly convinced that she would have had the strength to get on that helicopter.

'Bethany...' he prompted, shifting lithely beneath her.

She quivered, abruptly registering the hard thrust of his masculinity against her thigh. That shook her. She knew all about the mechanics of sex but she hadn't believed that he could be aroused again this quickly.

'And now you go silent.' A caressing hand curved to her sensitive jawbone. He smiled at her—the sort of megawatt-brilliant smile which clenched her heart and sent every alarm bell jangling. 'And you look so worried but also very sexy.'

He ran a fingertip lightly along the lower lip swollen by his passionate kisses, and she collided mesmerically with smouldering green eyes, felt her pulses leap. With his thumb he prised her lips apart and softly invaded the tender interior, and in shamed disbelief she felt a surge of heat quicken between her thighs.

'Forget the world outside these walls,' Razul instructed huskily. 'This is our world and nothing can threaten you here.'

Nothing but him. The acknowledgement pierced her deep. 'Razul...'

He leant closer and allowed his tongue to penetrate just once between her parted lips in a darting, highly erotic assault which made her every skin-cell tingle. 'I want you again.'

'N-no!' she gasped strickenly, snaking away from him as if she had been threatened with violence.

He tugged her back to him with easy strength. 'Would I hurt you?'

A tide of scarlet washed over her cheeks as she connected with the concern in that clear, candid gaze. 'Yes...' she lied shakily.

'There are many ways of making love—'

'And I don't want to know about them!' Bethany asserted feverishly, on the edge of panic.

Razul angled a highly amused smile at her. 'But you will. Come on...we will go for a swim—'

'A swim?' she echoed, in a daze.

'If I am to restrain my hunger for you, *aziz*, the equivalent of a cold shower becomes a necessity.'

'Oh...go ahead,' she said with helpless enthusiasm.

He threw back his handsome dark head and laughed uproariously. Before she could ask him what he found so funny, he sprang out of bed and swept her up into his arms in one powerful motion. 'We share everything from this night on,' he assured her.

'I do not need a cold shower.'

'But you deserve one, *aziz*. Were it not for my recollection of the ecstasy you found in my arms, I would now feel most deficient as a lover.'

'You're a perfect ten. Don't worry about it,' Bethany bit out acidly. 'Now will you please put me down? I am not one of those women who go all weak at the knees at the superiority of male muscle-power!'

He lifted her higher and ravished her tender mouth in a hot, hungry surge that left her dizzy and wildly disorientated. 'Now that *does* make you go weak at the knees,' he told her without skipping a beat, lashings of raw amusement in the wolfish grin curving his firm mouth. 'A perfect ten?' he mused. 'But who do you compare me with? Did you fantasise about me as well?'

'I have never had a—'

'What a little liar you are... stubborn, aggressive, sharp-tongued... It is as well I did not marry you in the hope of honeyed sweetness and flattery.'

'You married me to get me into bed!' Bethany spat back at him.

'But I didn't have to.' He smoothly disconcerted her with that cool rejoinder. 'I could have taken you to my bed in England but I chose not to put your powers of self-restraint to the test... You should be grateful—'

'*Grateful*?' she gasped, with clenched fists.

He gave her a sardonic glance. 'You would have failed the test. I could have taken you the first time I kissed you.'

Enraged, Bethany took a swing at him and a split second later her overheated body was plunged into cold water. Spluttering and splashing and gasping in shock, she recoiled against the tiled wall of the pool for support and clawed her dripping hair out of her eyes.

'I will not allow you to strike me. While you are my wife you will treat me with respect.'

In the moonlight he was a dark golden silhouette, standing barely waist-deep in the lapping water. '*While you are my wife*', she registered furiously. Always the time limit—not that that mattered a damn to her, for loving him did not close her eyes to the impossibility of a more lasting relationship between them. On the other hand, she bitterly resented his arrogance in believing that he could take what suited him from the institution of marriage and deviously cast aside what did not.

'Not only do I not believe in marriage, I do not feel like your wife and I do not want to be your wife,' she spelt out hotly. 'I do not feel *honoured* ... I feel used. Those ceremonies were a mockery and you needn't think that putting a ring on my finger blinds me to that fact.'

Razul moved towards her. 'So you feel *used*,' he grated rawly. 'But then what can tenderness mean to you? Only something more to despoil as you seek to despoil everything we share, with your narrow, closed little mind and your selfish, smug sense of superiority!'

Her whole body had turned icy cold and the angry colour had drained from her cheeks. 'I do not feel superior,' she whispered strickenly, devastated by the dark fury that she had unleashed.

'But you give me your body and nothing else. It seems I am not worthy of anything more. If our marriage truly means nothing to you, I was wrong to make you put that ring on again.' He caught her to him, splayed her fingers and wrenched off the slender band. He sent it spinning into the water in a gesture of vehement repudiation. 'It will lie there for eternity, for you would have to come to me on your knees for me to allow you to wear it again!'

It was crazy, but the minute he took that ring from her she wanted it back with a passion as strong as his repudiation. Narrow-minded, selfish, smug, she recited inwardly, her throat thickening with tears. Was that really how he saw her? That hurt; that really hurt.

'But I need no ring on your finger to licence me to enjoy what is already mine.' Before she could even guess his intention, Razul planted firm hands on her hips and lifted her up out of the water onto the edge of the pool.

'What are you doing?' she gasped.

'What *I* want to do,' Razul informed her rawly, pressing her knees apart with his hard thighs as he sank

CHAPTER EIGHT

BETHANY shifted in the comfortable bed and shivered convulsively with cold. Her arm was throbbing. She ached all over, she ached in places she hadn't even known she could ache, but, strangely, she felt drowsily detached from her physical discomforts and her mind was disorientatingly awash with a flood of erotic imagery.

She was remembering the hot, drugging glory of Razul's mouth on hers, the phenomenal speed at which her treacherously eager body had quickened to melted honey. She was remembering that savage joining as he'd sunk into her over and over again, remorselessly driving her to a pitch of excitement far beyond her wildest fantasies. She was remembering her own wanton ecstasy when he'd chosen to ditch all control and cool...and was shrinking inwardly from the shame of her own weakness.

Yet she was too honest to deny that she had gloried in that sensual intimacy and rejoiced in his hungry need for her and that, most of all, she had loved falling asleep in his arms, knowing that he was there in the night and feeling wonderfully secure in that sense of no longer being alone.

So, it had begun, she sensed wretchedly. This was what love did to you. It levelled your pride and betrayed your principles. It made a sane woman behave insanely. Her mother was an intelligent woman, but intelligence had not once prompted her to break away from her destructive marriage.

No, her mother stayed the course, apparently hooked on the pain and humiliation of possessing a wandering spouse. 'He's my husband and I love him,' she had told her daughter in staunch reproof in the days when Bethany had still been naïve enough to think that she should interfere. Escape to university had been a blessing, and in burying herself in her studies and carving out her career Bethany had gradually let the ties of home wane to their current level of occasional letters.

With a weak hand she tugged at the sheet, trying to warm herself.

Had she really protected herself all these years just to fall flat on her face for a male who was a sexual predator like her father? The kind of man who stoked his inadequate ego with female flattery and surrender, who made an art form out of lying and who was loyal to nothing but his own self-interest. But that *wasn't* Razul, she conceded grudgingly, her head aching fit to burst.

It was laughable to think of Razul as inadequate. In the ego line, he was as tough as old boots. He was also fiercely loyal to his family, not to mention being possessed of a nasty habit of brutal candour that was frequently grossly unwelcome to Bethany's ears. In fact, if there was anything you least wanted to hear about yourself, Razul was most likely to break the bad news, presumably in the hope that you would admit the flaw and work hard to eradicate it.

But not one of those virtues made him any less of a predator, Bethany reminded herself painfully. Indeed, that powerful character made him even more dangerous, for she saw now that it was that innate strength and tenacity of purpose which she found so very attractive. He was the only man who had ever stood up to her, the only man who had ever managed to penetrate her defensive shell ... and the only man ever to surprise her by constantly doing the unexpected, refusing to fall into the neat little pigeon-holes into which she had scornfully slotted all men from an early age.

So now she knew why she loved him. But that didn't blind her to the knowledge that all Razul wanted from her was that wild sexual oblivion which he had introduced her to last night. Only he wasn't prepared to admit that openly, was he? Presumably, if he did, his own moral scruples would take a battering. Marriage was much more respectable than an affair—which he could not possibly have got away with in Datar—but their marriage was *still* only a temporary affair.

It was becoming an effort to think, she registered, twisting her head back and forth on the pillow, her mouth as dry as a bone as she fought to concentrate. Her arm gave an unbearable twinge as she moved it, and with an effort, for she felt very weak, she pushed back the sheet and surveyed it with a curiously detached sort of interest. It was swollen and angry-looking, particularly puffy round the plaster covering Fatima's scratches. Blood poisoning, she decided, and she was probably running a temperature, which explained why she was feeling so cold.

She heard a door open. Had it been locked? She recalled his threat to lock her up and throw away the key and smiled with helpless amusement. She loved his drama, too. Her mind was wandering, she noted with faint irritation—she needed a doctor.

Razul appeared in her field of view, fully dressed in an exquisitely tailored dove-grey suit. In Western mode today. He looked devastatingly handsome but he shimmered a little indistinctly round the edges, as if she was suffering from some form of visual disturbance. She wondered dimly why he was carrying a laden tray complete with flowers, because he had the distinct attitude of someone who didn't know what to do with it.

'You are awake... are you hungry?' he enquired very stiltedly, hovering quite a few feet away and looking staggeringly awkward. 'I have brought breakfast.'

Doctor, she reminded herself, grateful that Razul would be rock-solid in a crisis.

He cleared his throat in the silence. 'Naturally you are awaiting an apology.'

Was she? Why was she expecting an apology? She couldn't imagine, and continued to observe him with glazed green eyes from the depths of the great, shadowy bed.

'I regret my behaviour last night,' he delivered, an arc of colour accentuating the strong slant of his cheek-bones and the brilliance of his dark, troubled eyes. 'I have no excuse to make for myself. I lost control. I lost my temper. I have never done this before.'

She just couldn't concentrate at all. Doctor, she thought again. 'I need a doctor,' she told him weakly.

'A doctor?' He frowned uncertainly at her.

She pushed the sheet down from her aching arm. 'See?' she pointed out.

The tray dropped with a thunderous crash of smashing china. She blinked in bemusement as Razul suddenly came down on the bed beside her in what could only be described as a flying leap. A flood of volatile Arabic rent the charged silence. He grasped her fingers in a death grip and stared down at her, immobilised by shock. Panic, sheer panic, she registered in astonishment, and then he dug out a mobile phone, but his hand was shaking so badly that he evidently hit the wrong numerals, because he cursed viciously and had to start again. Nor was the call that he eventually managed to make distinguished by any princely form of cool.

'Sorry to be such a nuisance,' she sighed in what she hoped was a soothing tone.

He said something in his own language in response, his English obviously failing him. He groaned something in a tone of anguish as he snatched up her night-dress and began to feed her into it. Then he bundled her very gently into first the sheet and then the bedspread and swept her up, wrapped like an Egyptian mummy. About there, she slid into a feverish state of unawareness.

The next time Bethany surfaced she was in a dimly lit room in one of those beds with rails round it and a drip was attached to her arm. She felt terribly hot and uncomfortable, and she didn't want another thermometer stuck in her mouth and said so loudly. She heard Razul speak and heard a female voice literally snap back at him, which struck her as unusual, and if only it had not been too much effort to do so she might have looked just to see what was going on.

The time after that, she wakened up as if she had been sleeping. Her arm was no longer painful but she felt incredibly drained. The same voices were still talking. She shifted position with a faint mutter over the weakness of her muscles and opened her eyes. Laila was standing over the bed on one side of her, Razul at the foot, and there was more than a suggestion of acrimony in the air.

'There you are,' Laila said with satisfaction to her brother. 'I told you she was only asleep...as did Mr Khan.'

Bethany frowned in astonishment at Razul. He looked as though he hadn't shaved in a week and had been sleeping rough. A thick blue-black shadow of stubble covered his aggressive jawline. His eyes were bloodshot, his suit crumpled, his tie missing.

'How are you feeling?' he enquired tautly, ignoring his sister.

'How long have I been here?'

'Almost two days—'

'The longest days of my life,' Laila groaned. 'Please tell him to go home, Bethany, before I am tempted to commit a crime still punishable by death...an assault on his illustrious person—'

'You will not speak to me like that!' Razul bit out, making Bethany flinch.

'No human being can go that long without sleep and expect to retain a sense of proportion... and what has happened to your sense of humour?' Laila demanded.

'You expect me to laugh when my wife has been on the brink of death?' he asked incredulously.

'Your wife has not been on the brink of death. She has been *quite* ill but not seriously ill. Now will you please go home before I am reduced to ignoble strategy? You know as well as I do what will happen if I inform our father of your current state of exhaustion. One tiny hint that his beloved son is not rejoicing in robust health and he'll *order* you home.'

'I am staying with my wife. While she is unwell, this is my place.'

'Please go home,' Bethany muttered, feeling horribly guilty for causing dissension between brother and sister, and even more dismayed by the news that Razul had not slept in forty-eight hours.

His facial muscles clenched hard. His dense lashes screened his strained, dark-as-night eyes but she couldn't help feeling that he was reacting as though she had stabbed a knife into his back. His strong features harshly set, he withdrew a step. 'If that is your desire...'

As the door closed on his departure Laila groaned, 'You should have wrapped that up a bit. Now you've offended him and it's my fault. Ahmed would be cringing if he heard me speaking to Razul like that, but for heaven's sake... I'm twenty years older, I've lived most of my life in London and I keep on forgetting that my kid brother will one day be our king. I always had a big mouth,' she muttered wearily, 'but he's been acting like an idiot since you were brought in—'

'An idiot?' Bethany echoed weakly.

'He was in a blind panic. First of all he wanted to take you to London because he wasn't convinced we could offer a sufficient standard of care. I told him he really would have something to worry about if you had to wait that long for treatment. Then he wanted to fly in specialists. Then one of the junior staff... a young *male*,' she stressed witheringly, 'accidentally came in here, and Razul went through the roof and threatened to take you home if you could not be adequately chaperoned and protected from such an appalling invasion of your privacy. He has not left your bedside for a moment.

'He has not eaten, he has not slept and there are four guards standing outside that door... Any minute now I expect the arrival of an official food-taster!'

Bethany stared back at Razul's sister, wide-eyed. 'Oh, dear...' she mumbled.

'Oh, dear, indeed.' With a rueful smile Laila sank down on a chair. 'Now, I can understand that he's been worried sick about you, but I don't understand why he's been behaving as though it was his fault that you were ill!'

Bethany dimly remembered that apology. A sudden attack of conscience had undoubtedly prompted his extraordinary behaviour. Her heart sank like a stone. She would have felt wonderful if she could have believed that his behaviour had stemmed solely from genuine concern and worry about her well-being.

'As if it could be. You had bad luck, that's all. How did you get those scratches anyway?'

'Fatima—'

'Does Razul know that?' Laila gasped.

Bethany nodded, locked into her own miserable thoughts.

Disconcertingly, Razul's sister burst out laughing. 'That piece of news makes everything I have endured worthwhile,' she declared with renewed energy, and stood up again to press a button on the wall by the bed. 'Your specialist, Mr Khan, will want to check you over. Are you hungry yet?'

'No—'

'Please try to develop an appetite,' Laila teased. 'If you don't, Razul will import your Dubai cook...and then the next thing you know all our rich patrons will expect to do the same. Actually I'm very glad you are here.'

Bethany gaped at her.

'What Razul does, everyone else does,' Laila supplied cheerfully. 'If he had flown you to London for treatment, our reputation as a hospital would have sunk without trace!' She turned from the door and grinned widely. 'I am also depending on you to give birth to the first royal baby within these walls, but *please* let us make a pact to sedate Razul in advance of the big event, because I will surely strangle him if he starts trying to tell me what to do in my delivery room!'

A royal baby? In mute shock Bethany lay very still. Laila was under the impression that this was a *real* marriage. Of course she was. Why should Razul let his whole family know that she was only a temporary aberration? There was no necessity when he knew that by the end of the summer she would be gone anyway. But his father knew the truth, she suspected. Presumably that was the only reason why he had allowed Razul to marry her in the first place.

Well, King Azmir needn't worry himself, and Laila was destined to disappointment this time around. Razul hadn't run any risk of making his new bride pregnant. Even in the midst of wild passion in that pool, now she came to consider the fact, Razul had not taken any chances. He had carried her back to bed and protected them both from any possibility of her becoming pregnant.

And why the heck should that hurt so much? It was only confirmation of what she had known from the start. They had no future together. So why, when Razul employed a little common sense for a change, should that common sense feel like the ultimate rejection? She ought to be delighted that he had not risked such a development. Why was her mind now throwing up embarrassingly twee little pictures of Razul in miniature?

Her nose wrinkled as her eyes burned. She grimaced, furious with herself. A long time ago she had known that the one real drawback of the celibate life that she had planned would be never, ever having a child of her own when she loved children.

As she loved him... hateful creep that he was, she thought bitterly, turning her convulsing face into the pillow and absolutely despising herself for giving way to her emotions. Just to think of Fatima and him *together* made her stomach heave. The woman was a maniac! And not one single word of criticism had Razul uttered when Bethany had told him who had inflicted those scratches.

Of course, it didn't matter to him that Bethany had suffered grievously at that woman's hands. That nasty piece of work with no control over her temper and murderous impulses was very probably going to be the mother of his children.

All of a sudden Bethany wanted to die and leave him so miserable and so tortured by guilt that he would be totally useless as a husband!

'I understand that you are not eating very much,' Razul remarked tautly.

'I'm just not very hungry.' In the twenty-four hours it had taken him to show up again and visit her, Bethany had sunk deep into her misery, and when he had walked through the door looking as grim and tense as she felt it had been the last straw.

'I can understand that...' he breathed in an even tauter undertone. 'But you must be sensible.'

The silence was oppressive. She turned her face to the wall. He *deserved* Fatima, she decided wretchedly, trying to hate him, but somehow that only made her own pain bite all the deeper.

'I made a mistake in bringing you to Datar,' he conceded heavily.

Bethany went rigid, and emerged from the tumbled cloud of her veiling hair with a frown.

'I believed I could make you happy...for a while anyway,' Razul framed even more tightly, ferocious tension in every lean, hard angle of his features. 'I know now that that was very arrogant of me...and stupid—unforgivably stupid. I allowed my passions to carry me away. I have never wanted a woman as much as I wanted you. You were my dream... In the name of Allah, I sound like an adolescent boy!'

With a harsh laugh of angry embarrassment he strode restively over to the window. 'I was naïve enough to believe that we could have this special time together and that it would cost you nothing. I had so little time left. I have no freedom of choice. I *have* to marry and father children. I am thirty. That is quite an age to still be single in my position...'

'Yes,' she whispered unsteadily, absolutely ripped apart by a depth of honesty that she had not expected to receive.

'You were my dream...' she reflected on a tide of almost unbearable pain; if only she had been. He had exquisite tact. What he was really saying was what she had known all along. She had been his sexual fantasy, the desirable conquest who had refused to be caught, becoming even more highly desired as a result. He had wanted one last fling with a woman who was not of his world—a strong, independent woman who would scarcely fall apart at the seams or make a fuss when it was over—and he had never at any stage contemplated that one last fling turning into anything more meaningful or lasting.

'If it were not for my family I would have you flown back to England, for that is what you must want now,' Razul intoned almost jerkily. 'But for their sake I ask you to stay for a little while longer. The too sudden departure of my bride would cause them severe embarrassment.'

Bethany did not dare look at him. The thought of being transported home immediately filled her with horror. Yet it was cowardly to want to put off the inevitable. 'This special time together'...why couldn't she have been the type of woman who could accept that? And suddenly, finally, she understood why she had not accepted it.

She had wanted more—all along she had wanted more, even when she'd been fighting with him and telling him that she didn't believe in marriage. She had had her dreams too, even if she hadn't acknowledged them. She had wanted him for ever, she had wanted him to love her, she had wanted him to prove to her that marriage could work between them against all the odds...and that was immeasurably more naïve than anything he had expected, she conceded painfully. Cinderella gets her prince, the ultimate fairy tale...who would ever have believed that prosaic Bethany Morgan could harbour such a dream?

'What is your decision? I must know,' Razul prompted very quietly.

Thank heaven for his fear of embarrassing his family, she thought. 'I'll stay,' she said unevenly, and fished around for a reasonable excuse. 'I can do my research.'

'Of course...your research,' Razul said flatly.

But that wasn't all she planned to be doing, Bethany decided with an abrupt flash of decisiveness which startled her. Right now Razul had the impression that the end of the summer couldn't come quickly enough for him. He had had enough. He had been disappointed.

He felt that he had made a fool of himself. He had given up on his *dream*. Well, she wasn't planning to give up on him that easily. If she was about to spend the rest of her life hopelessly in love with another woman's husband, she was going to have some worthwhile memories to take home with her! Right now he was *her* husband and the way Bethany felt—and she felt incredibly vindictive—Fatima was always going to feel second-best, and Razul was going to be languishing after his first wife for the rest of his days!

'I've been thinking a lot since I've been lying in this bed,' Bethany informed him in an impulsive rush, and there was considerable truth in the admission. Deprived of Razul for twenty-four hours, she had had time to come to terms with her feelings.

'You never stop thinking,' Razul said grimly, as if it were the worst possible offence that a woman could commit.

'My research means so much to me but it's terribly inconvenient that I don't speak Arabic,' Bethany sighed. 'You see, my research assistant *did*. That was why I picked him, and I realise that you're probably very busy but I was wondering if we could make a trip together—'

'A trip?' The apparently compulsive view beyond the window which he had been glued to suddenly lost his concentration. He swung back to her.

'Into the desert. So that I could get a real feel for the nomadic way of life. Of course, I would want the experience to be authentic—'

'Authentic?' he questioned, studying her with an obvious effort to conceal how stunned he was by the suggestion that she had just made.

'Basic and back to nature... just you and me against the elements without a cohort of guards and servants. They would rather get in the way of authenticity, don't you think?' she queried less confidently.

'But you would be alone with me,' Razul pointed out very drily, his black lashes very nearly hitting his cheek-bones as he surveyed her with compelling intensity. 'I had not thought you would wish to be subjected to such unwelcome intimacy.'

Bethany took a deep breath, her cheeks hotting up to scarlet as she studied his feet. 'When did I say it would be unwelcome? It's not as though I hate you or anything like that.'

A silence had never been so thunderously loud in her ears.

'You would trust me not to touch you? I am not sure I could withstand the temptation of being alone with you.' It sounded as if admitting that physically hurt him.

'I was hoping not...' Bethany licked her dry lips as the silence got even noisier and her face got even hotter. She was beginning to wonder if she was quite sane. She had the feeling that he was wondering too. Green light... then red stop-light, she recalled, writhing with mortification.

'You were hoping I would *not* withstand temptation?' he framed raggedly.

Dumbly she nodded, silenced by shock at what she had just told him.

Razul gave her the fright of her life. He groaned something volatile in Arabic and grabbed her out of the bed, drip and all, just as the door opened.

'What on earth are you doing?' Laila enquired in disbelief.

'I am taking my wife home,' Razul announced aggressively, as if he was expecting a fight. 'I will take a nurse too.'

Laila was struggling to keep her face straight. 'Honeymooners. You make me feel every year of my age.'

As his sister left to make the arrangements Razul enveloped Bethany in a smouldering golden scrutiny that

CHAPTER NINE

LATE afternoon, Razul strolled across the grass towards her, fluidly graceful in his desert robes but wearing that slight frown-line between his aristocratic brows which told her that he was about to be difficult.

'You are usually taking a nap at this hour,' he reminded her, tawny eyes sweeping over her where she reclined in the shade of the trees with a book.

'I'm feeling as fit as a fiddle.'

'You still look pale...and strained.'

Bethany bowed her head. Only a week ago she had dropped her defences, burnt her bridges and thrown herself at Razul's head. Never in her worst nightmares had she imagined sacrificing her pride to such an extent. And with what result? she asked herself, with the furious and bewildered resentment which had begun to rise in her over the past week.

For some reason, Razul had gone from that brief instant of seeming jubilance at the hospital into a cool, distant mood. He was extremely polite and remarkably attentive. He brought her flowers and books and visited her several times a day, but he might just as well have been a gracious host calling in on an ailing house guest for there was nothing more intimate in his attitude towards her.

'When are we going into the desert?' she murmured bluntly.

'Perhaps next month when the temperatures begin to fall. You could not tolerate the current levels of heat—'

'I am quite sure I could—'

'But then you do not know what you are talking about,' Razul incised with steely cool. 'And you will surely allow that I do? At this time of the year the desert is a furnace, and to undertake such a trip would be utter madness.'

Bethany set her teeth. 'You can have your own tent...if that's what's worrying you!' And then the minute she'd said that she wanted to crawl under the recliner and cringe. But the most deeply humiliating suspicion had begun to torment her. After she had transformed herself from an exciting challenge into a positive pushover at the hospital, had it then dawned on Razul that he no longer found her madly desirable? Was he now cursing the situation in which he found himself, longingly wishing that he could get rid of her and fervently embrace Fatima without delay?

Involuntarily she glanced up, and caught the feral gleam in his golden eyes and the grimly amused twist of his sensual mouth. 'Does your bed become lonely?' Razul drawled slumbrously.

She flushed to the roots of her hair.

'I am become a sex object. I do not find this role entirely unfamiliar. Other members of your sex have viewed me in this light. But you are my wife—'

'Temporarily!' Bethany lashed back, awash with furious embarrassment at the fact that he could read her so easily.

'And though I have no desire to be offensive—'

'But you do it so well, don't you?' she spat, fit to be tied.

'I am not your stud.'

'I beg your pardon?' Bethany was so outraged that she could hardly get the words out.

'You would like it very well if I came to your bed every night in silence and departed equally silently by dawn. You could have the physical pleasure without yielding me a single glimpse of your inner self. I will not be used in such a fashion. When you learn to talk to me, I will share your bed—'

'I don't want to talk to you... I don't want you in my bed... in fact I wish you'd take a running jump off the nearest cliff!' she launched at him, quivering all over with raw mortification.

'But I know that none of this is true,' Razul delivered with gentle emphasis. 'You simply cannot bear to be thwarted. Were you never disciplined as a child?'

Bethany's mouth fell open.

'I ask,' Razul murmured smoothly, 'because I threw such tantrums once... but I *was* disciplined. It did me a great deal of good.'

Bethany clasped her hands together tightly and slowly counted to ten.

Razul sank down fluidly into a chair opposite her. 'I would like a cool drink.'

Bethany lifted the iced jug beside her and proceeded to pour.

'And I do not wish to have it thrown at me.'

'Really?' Bethany breathed dangerously.

'I would hate to subject you to the indignity of being dumped in the nearest pool. Rumour of your paddling experience in the fountain on our wedding day has already spread beyond these walls.'

She went scarlet and counted from twenty to fifty in the simmering silence.

'That your temper matches the fire of your hair is no longer any secret.'

The count made it to a hundred at supersonic speed.

'Now what would you like to talk about?' Razul drawled with outstanding cool and a gently encouraging smile.

'Methods of torture and death,' she bit out shakily before she drew in a deep, sustaining breath and could bring herself to look at him again. 'You make me so mad sometimes,' she conceded, with a rueful groan.

'At least I do not bore you as my father bored my mother.'

'You said she left him before she died,' Bethany recalled abruptly.

His expressive mouth twisted. 'She is not dead.'

She frowned in astonishment. 'But Zulema told me—'

'I assure you that she is very much alive—the socialite wife of a prominent French politician and the mother of two other adult children.'

'Did your father divorce her?'

'She divorced him on her return to her family. My father was too proud to admit that he was a holiday romance which soured...thus the false report of her death.'

Bethany was fascinated. 'A *holiday* romance?'

'Laila's mother had died, leaving my father a widower with four daughters. He met my mother in Paris,' Razul explained calmly. 'She was young and rich and spoilt and she thought it might be fun to marry an Arab prince. My grandfather was still on the throne then—'

'Are you telling me that your mother was French?' Bethany interrupted helplessly. 'Christian?'

'Yes. Scarcely a problem. Over a third of the population of Datar is Christian,' Razul reminded her gently.

She had forgotten that fact. A century ago a large number of Christians of the Coptic faith had migrated from Egypt and begun settling in Datar. Their presence had led to a greater degree of religious tolerance and a smoother passage into a more secular society than was possible in many other Muslim countries. But she was stunned to learn that Razul was part French and, as if he understood her astonishment, he gave her a wry look.

'I resemble my father, not my mother.'

'How long were they married?'

'Longer than she desired for she became pregnant the first month. She left Datar when I was two weeks old.'

'Your father wouldn't have allowed her to take you with her,' Bethany assumed.

'She had no wish to do so. A half-caste child would have been an embarrassment to her. It was much easier for her to remarry without me in the picture.'

Half-caste? Bethany felt quite sick at the expression. 'Was that what your father told you?'

'You are keen to put all blame upon my father's shoulders,' Razul sighed, his dark eyes revealing his exasperation. 'He was deeply in love with her—an older man, perhaps not very wise to the ways of Western women but most vulnerable to so crushing a rejection, and that I, too, should be rejected inflicted the deepest wound of all.'

Bethany had flushed. But picturing that right old misery of a tyrant, as she had always imagined him, as a vulnerable, relatively unsophisticated older man, unceremoniously dumped by his bored young wife, took some doing. 'Have you ever had any contact with your mother?'

'Once. I went though my father warned me that it would be foolish.' His lean fingers tautened round the glass he held and he gave a rueful laugh. 'A skeleton rising from the grave could not have inspired more horror than I did. She does not like to remember that there was ever another marriage or another child because her husband does not love those of my race. In my presence she swore her servant to secrecy about my call.'

'What a hateful thing to do to you!' Bethany exclaimed hotly, appalled that any mother could have faced her son with such a repudiation, most particularly a son who, in spite of her desertion, had still retained sufficient generosity to seek her out.

'You sound as though you actually care, *aziz*.'

Bethany froze; her gaze collided with compellingly intense dark eyes and she glanced away at speed, guarding her heart, guarding her tongue. 'Of course I do. I wouldn't want my worst enemy to go through an experience like that!'

'I did not suffer so much,' Razul countered drily. 'I had a father who loved me and, by the time I was three, a stepmother who raised me as though I were her own child. I also have two younger sisters whom you would have met had our marriage not been arranged at such speed. Both are married and living abroad.'

'So you are the only son.'

'Which may explain to you why my father is so embarrassingly protective of me. Laila did not joke. I sneeze in his presence and he turns pale,' Razul revealed with wry exasperation. 'I have often wished that Allah had blessed him with more sons.'

'His *beloved* son,' she recalled Laila saying. It had not occurred to her then that Razul was in fact the only son that King Azmir had. Six girls and one little boy, who must have been more precious then gold-dust from the hour of his birth, but equally that same circumstance must have placed an enormous weight of responsibility on Razul's shoulders to be the perfect son and fulfil all expectations. Her hazy image of her father-in-law had taken quite a beating: not an old tyrant where his son was concerned, but, by all accounts, a loving, indeed over-protective father.

'My father began developing his famous distrust of the Western world after his marriage failed. He was unreasonably embittered by the experience. For that same reason I was educated here in Datar...'

Bethany almost groaned out loud. 'And then the one time he let you go to the West—'

'I met you.' Razul drained his glass and set it aside. A bitter curve twisted his firm mouth. 'And when the rains come and you leave he will say... No, I will not think now of what he will say.'

No doubt there would be an entire week of joyous celebration at the old palace and convivial relations would be fully restored between father and son. 'Of course ... he didn't want you to marry me.' She had to force herself to say that out loud.

'He did not.' Razul made no attempt to duck the issue.

'So why did you *do* it?' she whispered helplessly, understanding better than most the incredible courage it must have taken for Razul to defy his elderly parent. Arab sons honoured their fathers. Arab sons were expected to regard paternal wishes as absolute rules to be obeyed without question.

'I have already told you why.' Perceptibly Razul had withdrawn from her again, his hard-boned features harshly set.

'You wanted me that much?' Bethany persisted unsteadily.

'Do you think I make a habit of kidnapping women and springing sudden marriages upon them?' A shadowy glimmer of his beautiful smile briefly crossed his mouth. 'I hear you have already inspected the stables ... can you ride?'

The change of subject was so swift as to leave her breathless. 'Ride?'

'I ride at dawn every day when it is cool. Tomorrow, were you willing, I would take you with me. The desert is a place of wondrous beauty at that hour ... I would share it with you.'

'Not much point in us sharing anything, is there?' Bethany muttered tightly, suddenly attacked on all sides by a tidal wave of bitter pain.

'Because you will leave?' Razul rose to his feet. 'Defeatist as always, *aziz*. If I can live with this knowledge, why cannot you? And why should I wish to settle for some empty charade of a relationship in the time that remains to us? I want the gold, not the gilt. I will not devalue what we might have together as you would devalue it. We will do more than share a bed before you return to your world.'

Bethany breathed in deeply and leant back fully to take in all six feet two inches of him as he stood with complete poise in the brilliant sunlight. 'Ten days ago nothing I could say or do would persuade you to leave me alone,' she reminded him fiercely.

'Ten days ago, even one week ago, I was foolish enough to believe that your attitude to me was...shall we say...warming, softening, *thawing*?' Razul queried with galling amusement. 'But when I visited you here in your sickbed I learnt my mistake. We have discussed the weather although there is nothing to discuss. Does not a hot sun rise with every dawn? We have also discussed your reading matter, your research and world politics.'

'Have I been boring you?' Her face was as hot as hell-fire at that crack about the weather.

'You are far too intelligent to be a bore and your observations and opinions are always of interest to me,' Razul retorted gently. 'But, while you evade every personal subject and are scrupulously careful to show no more real interest in me than you might show in a stranger passing by you in the street, I feel we are still in a phase of courtship—'

'C-courtship?' Bethany slid upright, no longer able to bear the simple fact that he was looking down at her—both mentally and physically. He was driving her clean up the wall.

'You treat me neither like a lover nor a husband. You deny me all intimacy...except when you look at me.' His dark appraisal mocked her with an all-knowing sexual awareness that burned her right down to her toes. 'But, if I had to learn English to communicate with you, you too must learn the language which I desire to hear.'

'You want it *all* don't you?' Revenge, she thought bitterly. So much for the violins that he had played at the hospital when he had talked about her being his dream! He knew that if he touched her she was his...as much his as if he had a brand on her backside, she reflected furiously. But that wasn't enough to satisfy him—oh, no, indeed, he wanted to sneak inside her head as well and prise out her every secret so that his control was absolute.

'Have you ever doubted it?'

'Well, what do you want to know?' Bethany slung at him with a scornfully elevated brow. 'I have nothing to hide,' she declared.

'Really, *aziz*.' His tawny eyes danced with infuriating amusement. 'Are you so desperate for me that you must stun me with so immediate an offer?'

Bethany spread her hands in an arc of screaming frustration and then she caught his irresistible smile and began to feel foolish. 'You know how to send me up now, don't you?'

'I should have resisted the temptation . . . but then you take yourself so very seriously. You have accused me of so many ridiculous things. I look back in laughter now on my two hundred concubines, my other wife, your view of me as a potentially violent man . . . and more recently still the assumption that I am a sort of Jekyll and Hyde, who will turn into a monster within hours of wedding you,' Razul enumerated, and his mouth twisted. 'If I could not laugh I would be in deep trouble.'

Bethany swallowed convulsively. Now that he had reeled off all her accusations like that she was severely embarrassed by his tolerance. 'I'm sorry but . . . well, there was some justification for my suspicions.' She lifted her chin. 'My aunt was married to an Arab and she had a pretty ghastly experience. But I'm quite sure you are aware of that, since you had me investigated.'

A frown-line had drawn his fine brows together. 'I was not aware of it. The investigation only embraced your life over the past year, nothing more,' Razul stated very quietly. 'I too felt that I was intruding upon your privacy and sought only the information that you were free of any entanglement with another man.'

'Oh.' It was Bethany's turn to be disconcerted.

'Your aunt?' he prompted as they began to walk along a stone terrace under the trees.

Bethany's aunt was only seven years older than she was. She had been a frequent visitor in her older sister's home throughout Bethany's childhood. When she had been nineteen and studying for her degree, Susan had met an Iranian engineer at a party. Faisal had been utterly charming and seemingly as much in love with Susan as Susan had been in love with him. Their whirlwind romance had ended in marriage...*ended* in more ways than one.

'It was a *disaster* right from the start,' Bethany told Razul with stark emphasis. 'From the moment they were married he changed. He treated her like a prisoner. He objected to her clothing, her make-up and her friends. He accused her of flirting with other men. He tried to stop her going to her classes. He didn't even like her visiting her family. He turned against us too. In the end he was knocking her about and she was terrified of him... She had to go to the police.'

'And you cite this to me as evidence of a cultural gulf?'

'Wasn't it?' Bethany snapped.

'Surely such men exist within every culture? They are emotionally inadequate, irrationally jealous and possessive and they invariably turn to violence, do they not?' Razul drawled quietly.

Her tongue snaked out to moisten her dry lower lip. She was really quite devastated by a line of argument that she had never acknowledged before, because of course such men existed in every culture.

'He was a sick man and a dangerous man. It is fortunate that your aunt escaped him before he did more serious damage. But what was your family about in allowing so young and inexperienced a girl to marry a foreigner about whom they knew nothing?'

'He seemed so romantic,' Bethany said gruffly, recalling how reluctantly impressed even she had been by Faisal. 'He seemed absolutely devoted to her.'

'It must have been most disturbing for you to witness the aftermath of such a marriage.'

'Disturbing' barely covered it. Susan on their doorstep night after night, her haunted eyes swollen, face drawn, weight falling off her, all her youthful energy drained away by stress and misery and growing fear of Faisal's threats. It had been a nightmare period. But Razul was right, loath as she was to admit it. Susan could well have married one of her own countrymen and ended up in the same predicament.

'It was,' she agreed rather woodenly. 'But Susan did go on to get her business degree and she emigrated to Canada soon afterwards. She's actually a director in an international company now.'

'Has she remarried?'

'No.' Bethany almost laughed at the idea. 'She's very ambitious.'

'Your role model?'

Bethany flushed, thinking of the long talks she had had with Susan when she had fled to Canada two years earlier. Her aunt had hailed her as a virtual heroine for walking away from so dangerous and impossible an attraction. Susan had never regained her trust in the male sex. She was still very bitter about her two-year nightmare with Faisal, and for the first time Bethany fully acknowledged how deeply affected she herself had been by that same nightmare.

Faisal's apparent adoration of Susan had impressed her so much. The young Arab had seemed strong and caring, his relationship with her aunt before their marriage—in Bethany's adolescent eyes—seemingly the very essence of romance. Scarred as she was by growing up in the atmosphere of a bad marriage, Bethany had nonetheless been touched and delighted to see two people

really loving each other. She had been absolutely shattered when that relationship had failed as well. It had
seemed to her then that there was no such thing as a
trustworthy or reliable man.

Bethany bent her head, admitting, 'I do admire what
Susan's done with her life since that awful period.' But
she was no longer sure that she could admire her aunt
for allowing that one, admittedly ghastly experience to
turn her off *all* men.

'Some women manage to combine both career and
marriage,' Razul murmured.

'Superwomen, you mean... baby under one arm,
vacuum cleaner under the other and a mound of work
they bring home every night from the office!'

'Servants do make a difference. My sister Laila has
managed this combination most successfully,' Razul
pointed out. 'As soon as their youngest child began
school she embarked on her medical training.'

'How on earth did she manage it?'

'Strong will and Ahmed's support.'

Involuntarily Bethany grinned. 'I have this feeling that
Ahmed jumps every time Laila snaps her fingers.'

'This is true,' Razul conceded with a pronounced air
of reluctance. 'But he is a skilled and most kindly man,
somewhat in awe of my sister even after all these years.
She has broken many taboos in our family and he is very
proud of her achievements. They have a very happy
marriage, a true partnership—'

'I wasn't criticising Ahmed,' Bethany broke in uncomfortably, wondering why he was labouring the point
of his sister's blissfully happy marriage and successful
career to such an extent. If anything it made her feel
inexcusably and meanly envious.

'There must be a certain amount of compromise in all
relationships between men and women.'

'And I know who usually does the compromising,' Bethany muttered with the cynicism of habit. 'The woman.'

'You know that is not always true.'

'Well, it's true more than it should be,' she countered, thoroughly irritated by the persistent way Razul contrived to put her in the wrong and make her sound like some man-hating feminist...like Susan? she asked herself uncomfortably, seeing much that she had refused to see before. Perhaps her aunt had become her role model because she had not been able to respect her own mother for the treatment she withstood from her father.

'Are you telling me that there are no women who take advantage of men?'

Her teeth gritted. 'You don't give up, do you?'

'You need to be challenged, for you are very stubborn.'

Involuntarily her gaze connected with his brilliant dark eyes and her heart skipped an entire beat, her mouth going dry. 'And you are not?'

'This is not a competition to see who can be most inflexible.'

Still looking at him, Bethany felt a prickling of heat twist low in her stomach. She could feel her entire body tense with physical awareness. Her breathing fractured, a sudden stirring heaviness swelling her sensitive breasts beneath their fine covering, pinching her nipples into painfully tight little buds. She watched his stunning eyes shimmer gold and trembled, her heart pounding.

'Do not look at me like that,' he breathed raggedly.

Bethany smiled with a new, sensual consciousness of her female power and waited. She was not one whit discomfited by her own response when she saw it mirrored in him. On this level, she thought helplessly, they were equal. 'Why not?'

With a muffled groan he reached out and pulled her to him, sealing every inch of her to the hard, lean muscularity of his male heat and strength. Her senses swam.

Instinct took over. As his mouth came down on her softly parted lips a long sigh of satisfaction escaped her and a wanton thrill of excitement jolted her from head to toe, leaving her dizzy and disorientated and clinging to his broad shoulders to stay upright.

When he set her back from him the shock of separation was sharp. She focused passion-glazed eyes on him in bewilderment. He steadied her against the wall behind her and withdrew a fluid step, studying her with grim intensity.

'You learn quickly.'

'You're a good teacher.' A hectic flush lit her fair complexion as she registered his withdrawal. Suddenly she felt unbearably humiliated.

'But I was too impatient. I taught you the wrong things,' Razul murmured very quietly, and reached for her clenched hand, smoothing out her taut fingers and cradling them in his.

Scorching tears had flooded her eyes. She bowed her head, immobilised by her devastating weakness. She wanted him so much. It was as if there were a clock ticking inside her where her heart should be. She couldn't think, couldn't be rational about the concept of losing Razul, but she could feel the time they had left sliding remorselessly through her fingers like silky grains of sand. The inner strength she depended on was fast buckling into a kind of fevered desperation in which she told herself that she knew what she was doing, when she really didn't know at all.

'I want to show you something.' Retaining a purposeful grip on her hand, he trailed her back indoors with enthusiasm and drew her into one of the reception rooms. A basket sat on the priceless carpet. 'It is for you.'

She crouched down and lifted the lid, already knowing what she would find within—another kitten, a rolling ball of Persian fluff with bright eyes, the twin of the gift he had given her two years earlier.

'You kept the female,' he commented. 'This one is male.'

'Yes. Thank you. He'll be great company for her...when they finally get around to meeting,' she managed stiltedly.

The pedigree kitten danced across the rug, swung an ambitious paw at the strap dangling from the basket lid and fell over in comical confusion. Yet she didn't laugh; in fact her throat closed over.

A matching pair, male and female. He probably thought that she would let them breed. It would not occur to him that she might have had the female doctored and that this was one little male who would not become a father. Her cat was barren, just as her mistress would be, she reflected, gripped by a sudden stab of pain. No kittens, no children—and although it was a ridiculous comparison to make it brought home to Bethany as nothing else could have done that she would never, ever have a child of her own, because if she couldn't have Razul she would have nobody.

'You are thinking of the British quarantine rules,' Razul registered harshly.

She heard that harshness but was too distressed by her own emotional turmoil to question it. 'He'll be quite grown-up by the time he emerges from six months of confinement and comes home to me,' she mumbled tightly.

'Please excuse me...I have some calls to make.'

His abruptness disconcerted her. She sprang upright, painfully reluctant to see him leave her. 'Do you have to make them right this minute?'

'For what would you ask me to remain?' Razul angled a chillingly impassive glance over her. 'No doubt it is your wish that I make arrangements for the cat to be put into quarantine now?'

'No...yes...oh, I don't know.' Hurt by his visible reluctance to stay with her and wretchedly conscious of the ice in the air, she heard herself ask, 'What have I done...what did I say?'

The merest sliver of gold showed beneath the lush screen of his lashes. 'Nothing of import.'

Yet the silence stretched and buzzed like a razor-edge, honing her nerves to screaming point.

Awkwardly she cleared her throat. 'Did your father live here with your mother?'

'Is that not obvious?'

East on one side of the hall, West on the other. A his and hers set of rooms which were unmatched to a degree that might have been farcical had it not been the evidence of a bitterly divisive gulf which had never been bridged. 'I gather nobody compromised in that relationship?'

'My mother had no desire to go what she called "native".'

Bethany winced visibly.

'You flinch, but were you any more generous on our wedding day?' Razul condemned.

She paled and then swung her head up again with pride. 'You didn't give me enough time to adjust...you *have* to know that!'

His lion-gold gaze shimmered. 'What I know is that that half-hour waiting in the desert was the longest thirty minutes of my life,' he admitted in a growling undertone. 'Having undergone that, I was determined that we would marry without further delay.'

'Because I tried to run away...or because I seem to have this problem with you when it comes to making up my mind?' She worried ruefully at her lower lip, her wide green eyes unguarded and vulnerable as she stared back at him. 'The first four days I was here I lurched from one shock to the next, barely knowing *what* I was thinking or feeling. Everything happened so fast; I couldn't control it and I've never been in a situation like that before. It was unbelievably unnerving...'

'But not giving you time worked for me,' Razul responded without apology.

Yes, with hindsight she could see that it had. He had kept her on the run, emotionally and physically. He had battered down her defences and allowed her no breathing space and that constant pressure had been more than she could withstand.

'It would not have worked for me in England,' he continued with cool emphasis. 'There you would have closed doors in my face, taken the telephone off the hook, run away somewhere where I couldn't find you. And even here, now as my wife, you place outrageous barriers between us—'

'But I'm not your real wife, Razul!' Bethany reminded him, stabbed by an inescapable surge of bitterness. 'I'm only here on a temporary basis. You seem to forget that.'

'How *could* I forget it when you hold that belief between us like a drawn sword?' Razul demanded with a blinding flash of seething condemnation.

'What did you expect?' she retorted painfully.

Golden eyes flared over her in a shockingly sudden storm of dark fury. 'You play dangerous games in the name of pride,' he condemned. 'Allow me to make certain facts clear. We will not meet again after you leave. Our time will be over and there can be—indeed, there *will* be—no turning back for I will be married again within months. That was the promise I made to my father. I also gave my word that I would not contact you again, although I now see no room even for temptation on that count...your cold heart does not tempt, it repels!'

Caught unprepared, Bethany was stunned by the pain that his words inflicted on her. Every scrap of colour drained from her face. She swallowed convulsively, couldn't even suck air into her lungs, she was so devastated by what he'd flung at her. Her *cold* heart ... she would have given ten years of her life to possess such a gift at this moment, to have the enviable power to detach herself from her pain.

But anger came to her rescue as nothing else could have done. Bringing her to Datar had been an act of unsurpassed cruelty and she blamed Razul absolutely for the torment that she was suffering now. It would have been better by far had she never known what they could have together. No, she *didn't* believe that old chestnut about it being better to have loved and lost than never to have loved at all!

She threw her fiery head back and fixed glittering green eyes on him, bitterness consuming her like a fire raging out of control. 'Do tell me what sort of second wife you are looking forward to receiving...' she invited with shrewish sweetness.

Razul froze in shock, his golden eyes veiling to darkness. 'That I will not discuss with you—'

'Why not? Heaven knows, you have been so disarmingly frank about everything else! So go on, *tell* me. I really would like to know!'

A silence of savage intensity now thundered between them, vibrating with her challenge and his wrathful incredulity.

'She will be a very good wife by my father's standards,' Razul gritted rawly, breaking that terrible silence with a suddenness that shook her. 'If I am ill-bred enough to raise my voice, she will beg to know how she has offended me. She will not answer me back. She will greet my every opinion with admiration and agreement. She will never come to my bed without invitation. She will spend her days dressing up in Western fashions, watching television, shopping and gossiping with her friends. I see her now,' he breathed with merciless bite. 'Beautiful, indolent by nature and not very well educated, but she will give me children.' A slight tremor fractured that final phrase.

Bethany had closed her eyes and turned away. She was devastated, her bitter fury quelled by shocked disbelief at the fact that he had actually answered her, called her sarcastic bluff with a candour that was savage. In a daze she stood there, heard him leave the room. The kitten scrabbled at her feet playfully, and as her knees gave she sank clumsily down on the beautiful rug and watched the tiny creature frolic innocently around her without really seeing its antics.

The deep-freeze effect of shock slowly receded, and her mind began to work again. She'd heard Razul describing his second wife not with pleasure...*no*, not with pleasure but with barely concealed revulsion. He did not want a not very well-educated wife, content to gossip and shop and watch TV and treat him like a god who could do no wrong. That might be his father's standard of a good wife but it was not Razul's. *That*, she realised dazedly, had not been his dream.

Tears of released stress suddenly stung her aching eyes. She had wilfully misunderstood what Razul had been telling her from the beginning. He had told her that he had no freedom of choice and she hadn't listened. He had told her that his father did not want him to marry her and she hadn't listened properly to that either.

In King Azmir's eyes she was not an acceptable wife for his only son and nothing was likely to change that fact. The old boy might be a fond and over-protective father but the only way Razul had been able to win his consent to bringing Bethany here had been by promising that it would only be a temporary alliance. It had been one last chance for them to be together before he did his filial and princely duty by marrying some brainless bimbo and settling down to produce children.

Not *his* choice; not *his* dream. How could she have been blind enough to believe that Razul would go to such extraordinary lengths merely to get her into bed? She remembered his panic when he'd realised that she was ill, and his distress at the hospital, and the tears fell faster than ever. Maybe it wasn't quite love but Razul really did care about her and he had never tried to hide the fact even when she was being more of a nightmare than a dream.

She covered her face with splayed fingers and sobbed with noisy helplessness as she thought of that ring lying at the foot of the pool. He had been trying to show that he respected her, that even if the marriage couldn't last it didn't mean that it had to be a mockery.

His father was a horrible, mean old man, rotten with prejudice and as cruel as some Dark Age medieval tyrant, she thought wretchedly. Just because *he* had made a mistake and had been humiliated and hurt by Razul's mother, he had decided that Bethany was unacceptable, unsuitable and not even worthy of a meeting or a chance to prove that she could be the right wife for his son. It was just as well that he was suffering from ill-health. At that moment Bethany decided that, if she could get close to the old misery guts, the sheer shock of hearing her opinion of him would finish him off altogether!

As she rooted around blindly for a hanky one was planted helpfully into her hand. With a start she opened her reddened eyes and focused strickenly on Razul as he crouched down on the carpet beside her. 'Go a-away!' she sobbed, cursing the sneaky silence of his approach.

'I have upset you.'

Her teeth gritted as another sob shuddered through her. 'Why sh-should you think that?'

'I have never seen you cry before.'

'What did you expect after saying what you did?' she flared at him on the back of another howl.

'You drove me to it,' he grated unevenly.

'That's right... b-blame me!'

He pulled her into his arms and she went rigid. But the achingly familiar scent of him washed over her and her resistance broke with dismaying abruptness. She buried her face against his shoulder and struggled for breath.

'I should not criticise you for being the woman you are,' Razul whispered, not quite steadily. 'For if you were not the woman you are I would not want you.'

She sniffed. 'That's perverse.'

'Then I am perverse . . . what does it mean?'

She very nearly laughed. 'Stubborn, contrary.'

'We are both these things.'

'Quick-tempered, aggressive?'

'These too.'

This time she did let an involuntary gurgle of laughter escape her. 'A match made in hell?'

'No . . . never that, *aziz*. Although I cannot face the end of the summer, I will hold these weeks with you in my heart for ever.'

Any urge to laugh was instantly banished. Bethany horrified herself by bursting into floods of tears again. She had never been more miserable in her life. He smoothed her hair back from her brow and muttered soothing, incomprehensible things in Arabic as if he were trying to calm a distressed child, and she had the lowering feeling that he was totally at a loss as to what to say or do. For what was there to say? she thought tragically. Like it or not, the end of the summer would come.

'You are exhausting yourself,' he murmured, but she had the oddest suspicion that he was actually quite cheerful about the fact, which was, of course, a quite ridiculous idea in the circumstances and one more symptom of her seemingly ingrained need to find fault with him, she scolded herself fiercely.

'I want my ring back,' she mumbled.

'You did not want it before.'

'I'm not crawling for it either!' she asserted jerkily into his shoulder.

'I have never wanted you to crawl,' Razul sighed. 'Only to give us this chance.'

Her throat threatened to close over again. Dear heaven, why did he have to keep on saying distressing things like that? If she cried any more she would be suffering from dehydration! She drew in a deep breath to calm herself. 'I will.'

'You will have changed your mind again by tomorrow—'

'No, I won't ... I *promise*!' she told him frantically, clutching at him with feverish hands while the kitten settled into the folds of her dress and went to sleep, having given up on the hope of receiving any attention from either of them.

'But what has brought about this change in you?' he demanded.

'The thought of you with another woman...you idiot!' Bethany sobbed, wanting to kick him just as much as she wanted to cling to him. Did he need everything spelt out?

'You are jealous?'

'Of course I am ... do you think I have the feelings of a stone?' she accused in disbelief.

'Occasionally I have thought this,' he admitted gruffly, holding her so tightly that it was an effort for her to breathe, and no use at all for her to go stiff with outraged pride and attempt to peel herself away from him, because he was infinitely stronger than she was.

She subsided again, too exhausted by her emotional breakdown to continue a struggle against an embrace that she was thoroughly enjoying. She rubbed her cheek against his shoulder, comforted by the hard, warm feel of him. A strange sense of peacefulness was creeping over her, along with a bone-deep tiredness. She stifled a yawn.

'Am I allowed to carry you to bed?'

'Absolutely.'

He smiled down at her, and even on the edge of sleep she felt her drowsy pulses speed up and her heart accelerate. 'Unfortunately I am dining with my father tonight.'

She tried not to let her facial muscles freeze but it was hard. Although very possibly she did not have the right to censure King Azmir's decision. Her tempestuous emotions had drained away, leaving room for a little intelligent reflection. Maybe she was a genuinely unacceptable wife for Razul. Razul was half-French. He was not wholly of Arab blood. It was very possible that a British wife and the son who might eventually be born of such a union would not be acceptable to the people of Datar as the family of a future ruler. It was a thoroughly depressing suspicion but a realistic one.

Exhausted as she was, it was nonetheless hard for her to get to sleep. She was thinking helplessly of the empty, narrow life she would return to in England. The idea stirring at the back of her mind was madness, sheer madness, she told herself... or was it? She had to have *something* if she had to face that future without Razul, and lots of women managed to raise a child alone. But to deliberately bring a child into the world without a father... But then what else would she ever have of Razul? she asked herself fiercely.

She wanted his child, *his* baby. Was that so wrong? He would never know. What he didn't know couldn't hurt him. Two months...two months in which to become pregnant by a male scrupulously guarding against the possibility. It was a tall order but not an insuperable challenge, she decided, pitting her wits against the problem and coming up with one or two possibilities which made her smile to herself as she finally drifted off to sleep.

CHAPTER TEN

WHEN Razul saw Bethany walking across the stableyard towards him, his brilliant smile hit her like a shot of adrenalin in her veins. Crawling out of bed in darkness suddenly felt worthwhile. He caught her hand in his and introduced her to the inmate of every stable on the block before finally drawing her over to a doe-eyed mare whom Bethany cheerfully petted.

'You like horses,' he murmured in a tone of discovery.

'Very much, but I've only ridden a few times in recent years,' she confided. 'So I'll be a little rusty.'

'Did you have a pony as a child?'

It was an unlucky question. Her beautiful face shadowed and stiffened. 'Once...briefly. She was a real little beauty too. I had one wonderful season on her with the pony club.'

'I sense that I have roused an unhappy memory. Did an accident take her from you?'

Her mouth compressed and she shrugged. 'No...my father took her from me. He said he was only loaning her out to a very good friend for a week or two but I never saw her again.'

'He sold her?' Razul frowned with immediate sympathy. 'Perhaps the expense had become too much?' he suggested.

Bethany uttered a wry laugh and swung herself up agilely into the saddle, wishing very much that she had kept her mouth shut. 'No, it wasn't that. The very good friend was an actress he was chasing at the time. She had a little girl too. He wanted to impress her with an extravagant gift, and why go the expense of buying another pony when he could take mine?'

Razul surveyed her in clear disbelief. 'You are not serious?'

'Look, he bought the pony in the first place. Can we drop this subject?' she said tautly.

'No, we cannot. Could your mother not prevent him from such an act?'

She expelled her breath in a charged hiss. 'My mother has never tried to prevent my father from doing anything in her life...and if it was unpleasant she just ignored it. At the time she pointed out that it was his pony, not mine.'

Before he could press her further Bethany moved off, directing the glossy little mare at the gates that led out of the stableyard. Beyond the walls she reined in, her troubled thoughts put to flight by the view before her. The sun was a great globe of rising fire, sending shimmering ribbons of glorious colour trailing across the dawn skies. Fingers of light fell on the sands, turning them peach and scarlet and gold, dancing off stark outcrops of rock and casting mysterious shadows. The desert landscape, so brutally drained by the merciless heat by day, had an eerie and glorious beauty at sunrise.

'You were right,' she marvelled as Razul drew level with her. 'It looks fantastic at this hour.'

'I could show you beauty here at any hour,' he asserted with immense pride and confidence.

His world, his heritage, and he was so much a part of it—as untamed as a land at the mercy of harsh elements that could not be controlled. She searched his hard profile with softened eyes and an aching understanding. 'You didn't like the English climate much, did you?'

'It was a change...but it was very cold. Come on,' he urged.

But she took her time in following him on that gorgeous Arab thoroughbred he rode. The sleek stallion raced across the sand, rider and horse enviably fluid and at ease. She liked watching him and smiled, feeling like a burden when he came back to her. He looked guilty too. 'I forgot that you had not ridden for a while.'

And he wouldn't take off again on his own, no matter how often she told him that she was perfectly happy to pad along at her own unexciting speed until she found her confidence again. Eventually she stopped telling him, for she could hardly help noticing that he was in a wonderfully good mood, that quick, spontaneous smile breaking out with quite devastating frequency. She couldn't take her eyes off him. He cast a spell over her and no longer did she feel threatened by that. Tomorrow, next month, indeed the end of the summer, suddenly seemed a lifetime away. One day at a time, she promised herself.

'We will breakfast outside and I will make coffee for you,' Razul announced on their arrival back at the palace.

'The proper way?'

He grinned. 'The *only* way.'

Taking time out from the quick shower that she had promised herself, she headed down to the old harem quarters, stripped down to her bra and briefs on the edge of that ancient marble pool and climbed in.

'Great minds...'

She spun round and her cheeks flamed pink as she saw Razul smiling down at her from the side of the pool. Tugging off his gleaming riding boots, he went in still clothed. 'Have you seen it?'

'No joy yet.'

'It's a big pool,' he sighed ruefully.

She started to giggle, and once she started it was very difficult to stop.

'I could buy another ring,' he suggested hopefully as he waded through the water.

'I want that one,' she insisted, sitting down on the steps and hugging her aching ribs. 'Another one wouldn't be the same.'

'Well, then, don't sit there being lazy!' Razul shot at her in exasperation. 'Help!'

So she searched too, but it was Razul who literally struck gold with a relief that was highly entertaining. He snatched it up, grabbed her hand and threaded it on her finger with a lack of romantic ceremony which nearly sent her off into whoops again. He looked down into her laughing face and his stunning eyes flared golden in the sunlight, an expression of such intense hunger stamping his strong features that she blinked up at him in sudden stasis.

'You are so very beautiful . . . and so very undressed,' he murmured thickly.

As the sweep of his appreciative appraisal took in the flimsy bra and briefs which were all that interrupted his view of her gleaming body, only then did she actually recall that she was half-naked. Her cheeks warmed at the awareness but she made no move to cover herself. Indeed there was a wicked delight, she discovered, in standing there in the glow of his very masculine admiration.

He lowered his tousled dark head and pressed his mouth against the corner of hers, teasing, playing. The front snap of her bra gave beneath his deft fingers and her breath caught. In sensual shock she watched her breasts spring free, wantonly bare and full, her pink nipples pouting into taut buds even before he raised a hand to touch her.

'Don't you dare stop . . .' she whispered shakily.

He laughed softly, found her mouth and tasted her as if they had been apart for a century and he could not believe the joy of finding her again. Her knees wobbled beneath the onslaught. She strained forward, the throbbing tips of her swelling breasts rubbing with delicious friction against the wet roughness of his polo shirt, and he caught her to him with suddenly impatient hands, pinning her to him as he strode up the steps out of the water and swiftly to her bedroom.

The tip of his tongue flicked against the roof of her mouth, twinned hotly with her own in a highly erotic assault that made her senses swim. She dug her hands into his thick hair and kissed him back wildly, all the pent-up passion of her fiery temperament bent on entrapment.

It was like setting a torch to a bale of hay. With a savage groan he lifted her high against him and curved her thighs round his lean hips. Electrified by that primitive response, she did it again. He reacted with quite devastating enthusiasm.

He brought her down on the edge of the bed and ripped off his polo shirt.

She rested back breathlessly on her elbows, excitement snaking through her in a shameless surge, an even greater excitement than that which she had experienced on their wedding night for it was infinitely less one-sided. This time there was no fear of the unknown and no terror of her own responses, only an aching, tender need for his pleasure to match hers. She wanted to tell him how much she loved him without saying it out loud.

So she rammed back her own shyness and curved forward to unsnap the waistband of the skin-tight riding breeches he still wore. The palm of her hand rested against the hard, swollen bulge of his manhood as she struggled with the zip in sudden embarrassment over her own lack of expertise.

'I will die of frustration,' he swore, with a sound between an agonised groan and reluctant laughter, and then his patience gave and he brushed aside her inept fingers, dealing with the problem in one second flat.

She flung herself back on the bed like a willing sacrifice, every tiny muscle taut with helpless anticipation. Razul surveyed her with slightly dazed eyes, as if he was not quite sure that this was really happening to him, but he dispensed with the shrunk-fit breeches with remarkable speed and fervour, hauled her back to him and kissed her breathless.

He captured an urgently sensitive nipple in his mouth and her whole body jerked, a stifled gasp dragged from her as an arrow of clawing heat flamed through her, making her hips rise and her thighs tremble. Her own response was shatteringly intense. Her restive hands skimmed in torturous circles over the smooth skin of his back and then sank into his hair tightly as her temperature rocketed.

A hot fever of excitement seized her as he wrenched off her briefs. Never in her entire existence had she dreamt of wanting anything as desperately as she now wanted him. Her heart was slamming against her ribcage, the blood pulsating wildly through her veins. As he caressed an engorged pink bud with the flick of his tongue and the teasing graze of his sharp teeth, he found the most sensitive spot of all with skilful fingers and made her jerk and quiver and moan, thrown helplessly out of control, her teeth clenched, her throat extended as the hot wire of sexual tension tightened and tightened until she was convinced that she was in mortal torment.

'Now... now!' she pleaded.

'I must—'

Her glazed green eyes collided with smouldering golden ones; she felt him begin to pull away and then she remembered—remembered what he must not be allowed to do. 'No need . . . it's safe,' she gasped unevenly, hanging onto him with both hands in case he didn't get the message.

'Safe?' he groaned uncertainly.

'Absolutely...' Hoping to take his mind off the idea altogether, she lifted herself up to him and found his gorgeous mouth again for herself, and so enjoyed that rediscovery that she quite forgot why she had deviously embarked on it.

The fierce heat of him burned her as he spread her thighs. She was at a pitch of excitement beyond bearing and, at that first driving thrust, cried out in ecstasy, her eyes closing, her head falling back. Then he was moving on her and in her, answering a need as old as time with the hard, primal force of his sexual possession.

Her response was mindless, drugging in its completeness. There was nothing but him and the wildly torturous drive for satisfaction, and when one final electrifying spasm of delight pushed her over the edge she gasped his name and went spinning off into hot, quivering ecstasy. He shuddered violently over her and climaxed with a hoarse shout of pleasure.

They subsided in a damp tangle of limbs. She was in heaven, didn't ever want to descend to earth again. A tidal wave of love and tenderness flooded her, making her eyes sting. She curved her head into his strong brown throat and a long sigh escaped her. 'I have never felt so happy,' she whispered dazedly because it really did feel so strange.

'Nor I.' He released her from his weight and rolled over, pulling her with him so that she lay sprawled on top of him. '*Safe?*' he queried lazily.

Bethany tensed, not having been prepared for so immediate an enquiry.

But Razul was not tense. Indeed he was totally relaxed. He skimmed a teasing forefinger along her sensitive jawbone. 'I feel I should warn you that what I suspect you regard as safe is not a remarkably reliable method of birth control.'

'I'm on the Pill,' she lied.

'The contraceptive pill?' he questioned incredulously, and closed his hands on her forearms to tip her up so that he could look at her. 'But why would you be taking such a precaution?'

'S-skin problems,' she stammered, flushing scarlet.

'Your skin is flawless.'

'I got a rash,' she said defiantly.

'You should not take such medication for only a rash.'

'What is this... the third degree?'

'I think you should consult Laila... I will mention—'

'Don't you *dare*!' Bethany cut in, aghast. 'Is nothing sacred?'

'Your health is.' He dealt her a wry look of reproof.

Her colour fluctuated wildly. All of a sudden she felt horribly guilty for setting out to deceive him. She dropped her head again. He thrust an arrogant hand into her tumbling hair and tilted her reddened mouth up, his breath fanning her cheek as he caressed her lips tenderly with his. 'You are a very precious woman,' he told her gently. 'I would protect you with my life. Do not deny me the pleasure of looking after you.'

Nobody had ever wanted to look after Bethany before. Nobody had ever been too bothered about what might happen to her. Razul might as well have put a hand on her heart and squeezed it. She was unbearably touched and unbearably saddened too. To meet with such tender caring and know that she would lose it again tortured her, but she closed out that awareness with all the strength that was the backbone of her character. One day at a time, she reminded herself fiercely.

'It troubles me that you have had no communication with your parents since our marriage,' Razul remarked wryly.

A finger of tension prodded Bethany's lazily reclined body. Her brows pleating, she looked out over the desert

from the vantage point of their cliff-top eyrie. With
canvas walls on three sides, the structure was a highly
realistic replica of a traditional Bedouin tent, and it was
permanently sited on the edge of the palace gardens. Rich
carpets, fabulous cushions and a coffee hearth distinguished its cool interior. Over the past weeks she had
learnt to appreciate how very much the desert was still
home to Razul. This was where he came to relax towards
the end of a long day and recoup his energies, disdaining
all the many magnificent rooms in the palace.

Conscious that he was patiently awaiting a response,
Bethany shrugged uneasily. 'We're not close.'

'That is something of an understatement,' Razul remarked after a sizeable pause, and passed her a tiny cup
of coffee. 'For an Arab, the family is everything. It is
the very foundation of our culture and such strong loy-
alties impose often painful decisions and duties.'

Her face shadowed. Was their lack of a future the
most painful duty he had ever faced or did she deceive
herself? Since that day she had cried in his arms Razul
had not made any reference to the subject of their
eventual parting. Not once had he again revealed the
smallest hint of tension or concern on that point.

The past three weeks had been the happiest weeks of
Bethany's life, yet to maintain that glorious contentment she had had to suppress rigorously every
thought of what tomorrow might bring. Was Razul following the same unspoken rule or was it simply that he
had already reached a stage where he could think of her
leaving without emotion? Was indeed their whole relationship just some pleasant little fling which he could
calmly accept as having an inevitable end?

'Bethany?' he prompted.

'Oh, my family.' She grasped his meaning abstractedly, her fingers tightening tautly round the cup as
she struggled to repress her fears. 'Well, I have a slight
relationship with my mother and a non-existent re-

lationship with my father, and that really doesn't bother either of them.'

'I find that hard to believe.'

She gave him a rueful smile. 'I suppose you do. Let me explain. My mother believes that having me almost wrecked her marriage—'

'But why?'

'My father's first infidelity coincided with my birth. If you knew him you would understand why. He has to be the centre of attention, and naturally a new baby interfered with that need. But, looking at his track record over the years, it's obvious to me that he would have been unfaithful anyway.'

'He was persistently unfaithful?' Razul studied her face with a frown.

'He was forever walking out for some other woman.' Bethany shrugged again. 'And then he would roll home again and Mum would greet him with open arms. As I got older and understood what was going on I hated him for the way he treated her. It took me a long while to appreciate that, in accepting his behaviour, Mum was and *is* a willing victim. He's a very attractive man...physically,' she adjusted grimly. 'But he just uses her. She's his port in every storm.'

'Do you still hate him?'

'If I think about him at all, I guess I'm ashamed of him,' she admitted. 'He's got nothing but that surface charm to recommend him.'

'I had no idea that you had endured such a childhood,' Razul sighed.

'It wasn't that bad,' she said ruefully. 'It's just that I was never very important to either to them. My father isn't interested in children. If I'd been an absolutely adoring daughter like his absolutely adoring wife, maybe it would have been different, but, you see, I couldn't hide the way I felt about him . . . I couldn't pander to his ego as my mother did and I made him uncomfortable and resentful. He doesn't like me. Frankly, when I left home for university it was a relief all round.'

'I am sorry that I questioned your lack of contact with your parents. I did not understand the circumstances. But I wish I had known these things sooner. I would have better understood your resistance to me.'

'I wish I still had some of that resistance.' She was sinking helplessly into the depths of those dark, intense eyes which were trained on her.

'I do not wish it,' he responded with very masculine amusement, reaching forward fluidly to deprive her of her cup. 'This is how it should be between lovers.'

'Lovers,' she repeated inwardly, stifling an odd little stab of pain. Funny how Razul never, ever referred to her now as his wife or to himself as her husband, or, indeed, in any way to the fact that they were actually married. Funny how those surely deliberate omissions could now fill her with a sense of rejection and deep insecurity and, no matter how hard she tried, an ever present awareness that she was living on borrowed time.

He leant over her and her heartbeat thundered so wildly that she was convinced he would be able to hear it. Brilliant golden eyes flamed over her with primitive satisfaction, and she trembled, feeling the spreading languor of desire constrict her breathing and flush her skin. The level of awareness between them now was so intense that he only had to look at her or she at him and the heat surged, closing out everything else.

'Allah has truly blessed us with passion.'

A tide of hotter colour embellished her cheeks; her guilty conscience stirred as she shamefacedly recalled a certain three days just over a fortnight ago when they had not got out of bed at all except to eat, and he had no doubt come to the conclusion that he had been blessed by an absolutely insatiably passionate woman. And admittedly he did make her feel insatiable, but she had the sinking, horrible suspicion that Razul would be appalled if he were ever to find out that she had had a rather more scientific purpose for ensuring that he stayed in that bed those particular days, and that even now she was anxiously waiting to find out whether or not all that passion had metaphorically borne fruit.

'You are very quiet.' He skimmed a blunt forefinger along the ripe curve of her lower lip. 'What do you think of?'

Her guilty conscience attacked her, releasing a sudden, dismaying cloud of uncertainty. Had she made a very selfish decision in trying to become pregnant? If Razul ever found out he would totally despise her for it. Was it fair to bring a child into the world without a father and without a father's knowledge simply to give herself some comfort? It seemed to her now that it was anything but fair, and what would she tell that child when it grew old enough to ask awkward questions? That she had deprived him or her of his birthright and heritage?

'What is wrong *aziz*?' Razul frowned down at her.

He called her 'beloved'. Ever since she had discovered from a smiling Zulema what that particular word meant she had hugged it jealously to herself and tried not to think that Razul might use it as casually as some men used such endearments in English. She looked up at him with swimming eyes, studied that hard-boned, sun-bronzed face which was so terrifyingly dear to her, and her awareness of her own deception bit hard. He had been so honest with her from the beginning.

'Nothing—'

'That was not nothing which I saw in your eyes,' he incised. 'You are becoming homesick?' His usually level drawl fractured on the last word.

Home? She didn't have a home, she decided wretchedly. She had a cat in a cattery and three bonsai trees being lovingly looked after by her neighbour. Nowhere was ever going to feel like home again without Razul. 'No.'

'I think you are not telling the truth—'

She read the fierce tension stamped into his lean features and it frightened her. She could not bear to talk about losing him, had become an utter coward where that subject was concerned. It was as if talking about it would somehow bring the time closer and kill the happiness they did have. Now reacting to the sudden turmoil of her emotions, she reached up to him, smoothing unsteady fingers across his high cheek-bones and pressing her lips passionately, desperately to his with the tears still damp and stinging on her cheeks.

For a paralysing moment Razul was tense and savagely unresponsive, and then, with a hungry groan, he caught her to him with strong hands and ravished her soft mouth with hot, hard insistence, and it was a relief when she felt that wild, wanton need fill her with a drowning sweetness that locked out her ability to think.

But there had been something disturbingly different in their lovemaking, she thought dimly in the aftermath. Certainly her own heightened emotions had lent a painful and yet immensely greater depth to her response, and just as she was striving to work out exactly what had been different she was shocked back into full awareness by what happened next. Razul literally thrust her away from him, sprang up and began to dress.

The tension in the air was so thick that it brought her out in a cold sweat. The silence was unbelievably oppressive. Sitting up, Bethany drew her discarded dress against her, suddenly agonisingly unsure of herself. 'Razul?'

'This is how you would say goodbye to me. You still think of the end of the summer, do you not?' he demanded fiercely.

Bewilderment gripped her as she focused on the muscles rippling on his smooth brown back as he tugged on his shirt. 'What are you trying to say?' she whispered.

He swung round, his bronzed features a frozen mask but tension emanating from every aggressively poised line of his lean, powerful body. 'You still think of leaving... I see it in your eyes!' he grated.

'How can I help thinking about it?' Bethany was plunged into a vortex of all the pain that she had struggled to hold off for weeks and she lowered her head to conceal her anguish.

'I can no longer live with this hangman's rope swinging above my head. It is intolerable. You are like a curse upon me!' Razul bit out with an embittered savagery that cut her to the bone. 'But I will no longer endure this curse. I am leaving you.'

She was in so much shock that she could barely hear him. A *curse*? She was a curse? He was *leaving* her? But it's not time yet, she wanted to scream at him in torment, and she wasn't ready yet, not prepared, not able yet to face that severance. 'You are leaving me?'

'I should have thrown you onto that helicopter!' Razul seethed back at her. 'It would have been wiser to end it then than now.'

'And now you're running home to Daddy,' Bethany mumbled thickly, helplessly.

An expression of such naked and incredulous outrage flashed across his strong, dark features that she was transfixed. 'You are not *fit* to be my wife,' he murmured with chilling emphasis, his self-discipline asserting itself with an immediacy that cruelly mocked her own loss of control.

And then he was gone, and she was left sitting there staring into space, sick with pain and completely at the mercy of it.

CHAPTER ELEVEN

BETHANY lurched nauseously out of bed like a drunk and only just managed to make it to the bathroom in time. After she had finished being horribly ill she sank down in a heap on the floor and sobbed her heart out.

Razul had been gone a week—the worst week of her life—and she didn't know what she was supposed to do next. She didn't want to go home. She didn't want to stay. Most of the time she just wanted to die. In any case how could she even *get* home without that visa signed in triplicate which he had mentioned? She couldn't even leave Datar without his permission. Her teeth ground together at that humiliating awareness.

For seven utterly miserable days she had lurched between hating him and loving him, but it was extraordinarily hard to hate someone whom you missed more with every passing hour.

And she was pregnant. She had got her wish and right now there was a lot of repetition of that old adage about being careful about what you wished for washing around in her mind. Her breasts ached and her stomach heaved every morning, and somehow there was no joy in the discovery that she was expecting the baby of a male who had rejected her on the cruellest, most inexcusable terms. She had thought that she *knew* Razul and in the space of minutes had been forced to face the fact that she did not know him at all!

He had been wildly infatuated with her but now that had burnt out. Once her mystery and challenge had gone, the pleasant little fling had run its course. After all that specious talk about her being precious and *beloved* he had rejected her and gone home to that hateful, vicious, nasty old man, and she now saw very clearly the resemblance between Razul and his hateful father. She had let herself be used and this was her reward and it served her right, didn't it? But, unsurprisingly, lashing that hard reality home to herself only made her feel more wretched than ever.

It was a couple of hours later that Zulema came to tell her that the Princess Laila was waiting for her downstairs. 'Tell her I'm not well,' Bethany instructed, and then groaned, recalling that Razul's sister was a doctor. 'No, tell her I'm very sorry but I don't want to see anyone right now.'

Zulema's dismay was unhidden. 'This will cause very grave offence, my lady.'

Her mistress reddened, recalling Laila's kindness to her while she had been in hospital. It wasn't Laila's fault that her brother was a creep of the lowest denomination or that Bethany was still incomprehensibly and insanely attached to that same creep. In fact, maybe she could mention that visa problem to Laila and employ her as a go-between.

Laila stood up as soon as she entered the room. 'You will be wondering why I am here.'

'Yes.'

'You look unhappy.' Laila surveyed her pallor and shadowed eyes with grim satisfaction.

'All I want now is to go home,' Bethany stated tightly.

'But if you are pregnant you cannot possibly go home,' Laila said very drily.

The assurance with which the older woman made that statement shattered Bethany. She found herself staring back at Laila in wide-eyed dismay. How on earth could she know or even suspect such a secret?

Razul's sister gave a humourless laugh. 'Bethany... you cannot walk into a chemist in the centre of Al Kabibi and purchase a pregnancy test and expect it to remain a secret. Naturally you were recognised, naturally such an interesting purchase was eagerly noted and discussed—'

'Discussed?' Bethany repeated strickenly.

'Our family may not suffer from the embarrassing intrusion of television crews and tabloid reporters in Datar but then our people have no need of such devices to know what we do. This is a small country and Datari society rejoices in a most effective form of the bush telegraph. The chemist will have been on the phone to his wife as soon as the door shut behind you, and she will have phoned all her friends while he was phoning his friends to share this exciting titbit, and within days everybody who is anybody hears of your interesting purchase. Had you wanted to maintain secrecy, you should have called me.'

Bethany's legs wouldn't hold her up any more. Wordlessly, clumsily, she sank down on the chair behind her.

'I gather the test proved positive.' Laila sighed. 'Razul must be told.'

'*No!*' she gasped in horror.

'Well, if you do not tell him I will,' Laila informed her with flat impatience. 'It is none of my business that you have driven my brother from you. I do not like you for it but the fact that you may be carrying the next heir to the throne of our country overrides all other considerations, and if you do not accept that fact you are indeed a very foolish woman!'

Bethany was paper-pale and furious. 'I did not drive your brother anywhere! He left *me!*'

Laila looked angrily contemptuous. 'I am aware that *you* want to leave him. He told me that—'

'He was lying!'

'My brother does not tell lies—'

'But then you don't know the promise he made to your father, do you?' Bethany slung back with abrasive bitterness as she rose to her feet again.

'I do know that he promised that if the marriage didn't work out he would remarry without argument or fuss.'

'But you don't know that our marriage wasn't a real marriage, do you?'

'What on earth are you talking about?' Laila enquired impatiently. 'Did not my brother wait two years to win my father's permission to marry you?'

'But only temporarily, because that's all your father would agree to...and what does that matter anyway now?' Bethany demanded unsteadily. 'Razul has walked out on me—'

'Temporarily? What nonsense are you talking? Razul loves you. *Everyone* in Datar knows how much Razul loves you!' Laila asserted with complete exasperation. 'In the end everyone also supported his right to choose his own bride, and you were a very popular choice because you are from the West. Many find this glamorous and also encouraging proof of Datar's new liberal image.

'It is true that my deeply pessimistic father was stubbornly set against such a marriage, but only because he was afraid Razul would be hurt as he was hurt...that you would find our culture impossible to adapt to and that the marriage would end in divorce as his did.'

Bethany licked her wobbling lower lip, frozen to the carpet by shock. 'Razul doesn't love me—'

'Of course he blasted well loves you, you stupid woman!' Laila shot at her with raw impatience. 'And now he's undergoing the tortures of the damned listening to my father miserably bemoan the fact that he ever agreed to him marrying you! What the hell do you think it is like for Razul right now? His romantic, fairytale marriage has gone down the tubes so fast he feels a complete failure, and he feels he's let the whole family down by marrying you, *and* he's got my father muttering "I told you so" at every available opportunity...so don't you dare talk about— leaving him!'

A strangled sob punctuated Laila's last words. She turned away, visibly fighting to conceal her distress. Bethany was reeling with shock. Was it possible that she had somehow misunderstood Razul about the temporary nature of their marriage? She so badly wanted to believe what she was hearing that she was dizzy.

'I am sorry to have called you stupid...' Laila said stiltedly, having firmly reinstated her usual self-command. 'But I love my brother very much and I cannot bear to see him in such pain.'

'I love him too,' Bethany managed in a wobbly voice. What had he said? Something about being unable to live with this rope hanging over his head? But he had always behaved as though he didn't expect her to stay... hadn't he? But then that didn't necessarily mean that he didn't *want* her to stay, did it? It might only suggest that he was very insecure about her feelings for him...

'Then what the heck is going on between the two of you?' Laila demanded blankly. 'I don't understand.'

Ten minutes later Bethany was rigidly seated in Laila's chauffeur-driven Mercedes. 'If your brother shoots me down in flames,' she warned shakily, 'you do understand that it will be my turn to call *you* a very stupid, foolish woman?'

Laila laughed with amusement. 'That is an opportunity you will be denied.'

Bethany wished she had that confidence. Could Razul have left her because he believed *she* was planning to leave *him*? That pride—that incredible pride of his, she recalled painfully as her fingers knotted tightly together on her lap.

'Ah, my father's secretary,' Laila announced, waving an imperious hand in the echoing foyer of the old palace as Mustapha trod towards them looking most reluctant to respond to that gesture. He avoided looking at Bethany altogether.

'Mustapha will take you to my brother,' Laila informed her.

Mustapha turned pale, his jaw-line stiffening. 'I regret to say—'

Laila murmured something low-pitched and brief in Arabic. Whatever it was, it had an extraordinary effect on Mustapha. His compressed mouth fell wide, and he flushed and shifted from one foot to the other in clear perturbation.

'Yes, indeed,' Laila sighed. 'If I were you, I would endeavour to circumvent such instructions. I would practise true diplomacy.'

It suddenly sank in on Bethany that Razul had already given instructions that if his wife should show up she was to be shown the door again. She began turning on her heel, white with furious humiliation, but Laila caught her arm and hissed in a fierce undertone, 'Do not be foolish, Bethany. My father is furious with you. This is his command. As far as he is concerned you have ditched his beloved son and a whipping three times a day would be too good for you!'

With a smile of reluctant amusement Mustapha inclined his head to Bethany and politely asked her to follow him. But what possible point was there in even approaching Razul if King Azmir was still so bitterly hostile to her? Her heart had sunk like a stone.

In silence Mustapha escorted her deep into the bowels of the palace. He halted outside a courtyard, ducked his head as if to check that it was unoccupied, and murmured, 'Please wait here, my lady. I believe Prince Razul is with his father.'

The courtyard contained a very elaborate and large conservatory. Unable to stay still, Bethany wandered into it and was astonished to feel the temperature-controlled cool of the interior, and even more astonished to lay eyes on the glorious collection of bonsai trees displayed on a series of ornamental plinths within. She focused first on a miniature forest of pine trees, and then, reached out a reverent hand towards an ancient-looking and gnarled Acer barely thirty inches tall, quite dumbstruck with admiration.

'Do not touch!' a harsh voice rapped out at her.

Bethany very nearly leapt out of her skin. She spun around and only then noticed the elderly man seated in a chair by a bench in the far corner. Clad in an old apron, with a pair of scissors clenched in one hand, he almost stared her out of countenance, so visibly infuriated was he by the interruption.

'I'm sorry. I should have known better but it looked so beautiful ... you see, I have some at home. They're my hobby.'

The fierce dark eyes narrowed fulminatingly. 'Bonsai trees?'

'Yes. I'm so sorry I interrupted you. Please excuse me.' A rather ghastly suspicion was beginning to cross Bethany's mind. Those dark, deep-set eyes, those level brows ...

'I do not excuse you.'

The rather ghastly suspicion was decidedly confirmed by that tone of hauteur. Bethany stilled, the colour draining from her cheeks.

'You are the wife of my son,' he pronounced through compressed lips. 'Why do you come here?'

Bethany tried and failed to swallow the constriction in her throat. 'I ... I wanted to see Razul—'

'Why should you want this?' King Azmir demanded harshly.

Her eyes burned, her tongue cleaving to the roof of her dry mouth.

'Why?' He repeated the question with grim emphasis.

Bethany hovered, tears of stark pain suddenly welling up in her eyes. 'Because I love him!' she finally bit out, thrusting her chin in the air.

He frowned at her, clearly taken aback by the announcement.

'And I believe I could make him happy...that is if he wants me to,' she adjusted unevenly.

'Then why are you not making him happy?'

'I would rather discuss that with him,' Bethany said stiffly.

Her father-in-law shook his head in exasperation. 'I do not like my son to be upset.'

'If you will excuse me for saying so, your son is very well able to look after himself,' Bethany murmured.

'Not when he marries a woman he cannot persuade to stay with him,' he retorted brusquely.

'I will stay.'

'Then why is he here and not with you?'

'I thought I couldn't stay. I thought that you...wouldn't accept me as his wife,' Bethany stated tautly.

'Do you not think that that is a most peculiar belief to hold when I agreed to the marriage?' he pointed out rather more gently.

'But that's nonetheless what I believed.'

'Is my son's English so poor?'

'In certain moods he is not the soul of clarity,' she muttered tightly.

Her companion studied her for several unbearably long seconds, and then he threw back his head and laughed with rich appreciation. 'Tell me about your trees,' he invited.

In a daze she began to do so and then he moved a silencing hand. She followed the path of his gaze and went rigid when she saw Razul standing in the doorway, his dark features frozen with incredulity.

'Take your wife home, my son, and borrow a dictionary,' his father urged him, with a wry look of amusement.

A tide of dark colour obscured Razul's hard cheek-bones, which were more prominent than they had been a week earlier. His lips parted and then, as he clearly thought better of comment, compressed into a bloodless white line. He inclined his head then strode back out of the conservatory. Hurrying in his wake, Bethany could barely keep up with that long, ferocious stride. They were out of the palace in five minutes flat and she was out of breath.

'A car will convey you home,' Razul informed her.

'Are you coming too?'

'No.'

He very badly wanted to know what had passed between her and his father but she sensed that torture would not have driven him to request an explanation. He wouldn't even look at her. She searched that coldly clenched profile and decided that it was not imagination which made her think that he had lost weight since she had last seen him. A Mercedes drew up.

'I'm sorry I insulted your father,' Bethany confided in a rush.

'We have nothing more to say to each other.' He turned fluidly on his heel.

'I'm pregnant,' she revealed dulcetly as she slid into the waiting car and slammed the door. The car drew off within seconds.

She glanced back over her shoulder. Razul was standing where she had left him, wearing an arrested expression of extreme shock. Well, whatever happened, she had had no choice but to tell him, and no doubt it was just one more messy complication, she reflected miserably, and, moreover, a complication that *she* was wholly responsible for creating. How stupid she had been—how unutterably stupid. Razul regretted their marriage now and she would just have to take that on the chin. However, her attempt to apply common sense to their problems only confused her more, for she could not imagine what could possibly resolve the situation that they were now in.

She was feeling a bit dizzy when she got back to the palace, so she went to her room. She had barely lain down when the door went flying open. Zulema stole one startled glance at Razul's furious face and scurried out past him at speed. Pierced to the heart by that dark fury, Bethany closed her burning eyes.

'Tell me that what you said is not true,' Razul breathed rawly.

'I'm afraid it is and it's all my fault. I suppose you want to strangle me and right now I want to strangle myself,' Bethany whispered with painful honesty. 'I lied to you when I said I was on the Pill. I deliberately set out to get pregnant, and I did feel bad about deceiving you, but not bad enough until it was too late—'

'Why did you lie?' Razul broke in roughly.

'I wanted a baby,' she muttered painfully.

'Without a father?' he gritted with contemptuous distaste. 'I have read about such women in your newspapers.'

'Well, I wasn't one of them! I wanted you too,' Bethany confided miserably. 'And if I couldn't have you the baby was the next best thing. I just don't know what came over me. It was a crazy, stupid thing to do. I knew you didn't want me to become pregnant.'

'I assumed *you* would not want to become pregnant.' Razul sounded desperately strained. 'Nor would I have risked such a development, not with the lesson of my own childhood behind me.'

Shock was settling in on him hard. She knew how he felt. Her own head was whirling in ever more torturous circles, for she could see no easy way out for either of them. She guessed that if she had a girl it would be all right for her to leave, but suppose she had a boy? And why did his father have to accept her when it was too late to make any difference? How much had his hostility towards their marriage contributed to Razul's rejection of her?

'You said...you said you wanted me too,' Razul remarked rather unsteadily.

'Yes,' she said equally unsteadily. 'My timing is very off, isn't it?'

'How deep does this wanting of me go?'

Her nose wrinkled. 'Miserably deep.'

'I need the dictionary.'

'I love you...all right?' she flung at him with sudden defensive aggression, her anguished eyes flying wide.

'But you are most unhappy about it, and no doubt if you are unhappy about it for long enough you will soon overcome such unwelcome feelings altogether and feel a strong sense of achievement,' Razul assumed with dark fatalism.

Bethany sat up. 'Is that what you're hoping for?'

'I am sure it is what you are hoping for—'

'And since you are always so sure that you know what I want, how could you possibly be wrong?'

'I already know that you have good reason to have little faith in marriage. I also know that you are devoted to your career. I cannot blame you for these facts. But last week, when I believed we were happy and that there was hope for us, I was devastated to realise you were *still* thinking of leaving me—'

'Razul...you left me with the impression that I *had* to leave at the end of the summer...no matter how either of us felt!'

'That is not possible. I was entirely honest with you,' Razul countered tautly.

'I believed that your father had only agreed to a temporary marriage between us,' Bethany spelt out. 'For heaven's sake, who was it told me on our wedding day that he would divorce me at the end of the summer and take another wife?'

'But this was when you'd accused me of deceiving you into marriage and made it clear that you wanted your freedom back and I said nothing that was not the truth,' Razul defended himself. 'I promised my father that—'

'You would remarry *if* our marriage failed?' At his frowning nod of assent she was ready to explode. 'You know something, Razul? You embarked on our marriage with so much pessimism you deserve everything that's gone wrong!'

'It was not pessimism. I did not believe that I had much hope of you staying with me—'

'Pessimism,' she said again.

'And naturally I had to be frank on this subject with my father—'

'Instead of keeping your mouth shut...you turned him right off me, didn't you? And you kept on saying things to me like "one last chance to be together", and you mentioned the end of the summer with such frequency that it became firmly fixed in my head as the date of my expected departure!'

His lean hands were clenched into feverish fists. 'Naturally I had to prepare myself for that departure—'

'But I didn't want to depart...I wanted to stay,' she whispered vehemently.

'Your career—'

'Stuff my career!' she raked at him, out of all patience.

Breathing fast, he studied her with painful but silent intensity.

'Just why were you so convinced that I would leave?' Bethany pressed furiously. 'Was it because that was what you really wanted to happen?'

His strong jaw clenched hard. 'I did not feel I could offer you enough to make the sacrifice of your other life worthwhile,' he proffered in a stifled and driven undertone.

All the anger in her was instantly doused. She could not doubt that sincerity. She lowered her fiery head, and

there was an enormous lump in her throat. She blinked
back tears. If he saw them, his pride would be savaged.

'All you have to offer me is yourself,' she managed
gruffly. 'And that is enough for me. I happen to love
you a lot. I can't even imagine my life without you now,
and you know...I don't even know whether that pleases
you or not.'

'It pleases...it overwhelms,' he muttered unevenly.

The silence went on endlessly. She heard his breath
catch, listened to him swallow convulsively.

'Does that mean you love me?' she finally dared to
ask.

'I have always loved you,' he said thickly. 'Surely you
know this well?'

'Oddly enough, no, because you never quite got
around to mentioning it,' she mumbled, then looked up,
and her impressionable heart spun like a merry-go-round
as her gaze collided with the deep, inner glow of those
burning golden eyes trained compellingly on her. 'I
honestly believed you had struck this devil's bargain with
your father that meant we could only be together for a
little while.'

'I was prepared to accept a little while if that was all
I could have.'

'I have a lifetime to offer.'

'And a baby,' Razul remarked abstractedly, as if that
fact was only now sinking in. 'This news astonishes me.
I can hardly believe it.'

'You're not even a bit annoyed that I lied the way I
did?'

'How could I be?' A blazing smile suddenly drove the
last evidence of strain from his lean features. He strode
across the room, came down on the edge of the bed and
breathed with unhidden emotion, 'What greater proof
of your love could you give me than to desire my child?'

'True,' she agreed, giving up on a seemingly un-
necessary need to appear remorseful.

'I thought you knew how much I loved you. I thought my love was embarrassingly obvious,' he confessed in a sudden surge of explanations. 'What did you think I was telling you in the hospital when I said that you were my dream?'

'I thought it was only—well...sex.' She flushed as she admitted it, finding fault with her own cynicism.

'In truth I am severely challenged being this close, to restrain my desire for you,' Razul murmured, with a rueful quirk of his sensual mouth. 'But nothing less than love would have driven me to lure you out here and browbeat you into a marriage within days. All I wanted was the chance to prove that I could make you happy—'

'And you had to fight your father for that chance—'

'I fell very deeply in love with you two years ago.'

Her eyes swam. 'I couldn't admit that I felt the same way. I was too scared.'

'My father was pressing me to choose a bride when he heard rumours about you. He confronted me and I told him that you are the one I love.'

'You are the one'... She rested her head against a broad shoulder and tightened her arms around him.

'The only woman I would ever love, the only woman I wanted to marry. He was profoundly shocked. He reasoned, he threatened and then he gave in with very bad grace and forecast disaster—'

'Misery loves company,' Bethany slotted in, but she was shaken by the awareness that he had fought for her, risking...indeed expecting to suffer ultimate rejection and his father's righteous censure.

'I am miserable no longer. And I do not even have to work out a subtle approach to the subject of having children. You have done it all for me.' With a glittering smile of slumbrous amusement Razul pressed her down onto the pillows. 'Three solid days in bed... I admire such strong commitment to a goal as much as I revelled in your passion. And this week—it has been the longest, most agonising week of my life.'

'Did your father say "I told you so"?'

'No...he was morosely sympathetic, which was worse. He asked me how he could blame me for making the same mistake that he did.' Razul grimaced at the memory.

'Didn't he ever want to meet me?' Bethany asked tautly.

'You were to meet after our wedding, but you were in such a mood, how could I risk it?'

Guilty recollection supplied her with a memory of the strained phone call that Razul had been engaged in when they'd arrived back here the day of the wedding. 'I'm sorry, but I was in shock.'

'He was too... The marriage was not to take place for some weeks but I lost my nerve to wait.' A faint line of colour had accentuated Razul's hard cheek-bones. 'I should have waited,' he conceded. 'I should have had more patience.'

'I'm not sure patience would have worked with me,' she admitted. 'But why did you stop mentioning the fact that we were married?'

'I believed that constantly reminding you that we were man and wife was making you feel trapped. I wanted you to see that we could be truly happy. But how will you manage without your work?'

She thought about it and smiled. 'I shall probably start writing books...but not right now. Maybe you find it hard to accept but I was a workaholic so long simply because there was nothing else in my life, and now there are lots of other things I'd like to take time out to enjoy.'

'Will you find occasionally entertaining foreign dignitaries very boring?'

'No.'

'My father does not like to be troubled with these duties unless the guests are personal friends. Furthermore, many men bring their wives these days and my father is not accustomed to such gatherings.'

'I think I could quite enjoy myself playing hostess. It would beat the hell out of watching TV and gossiping,' she said wickedly. 'Was it Fatima who was lined up to take my place?'

Razul frowned. 'That is a joke in very bad taste,' he scolded with mock sobriety. 'No. My father did once consider Fatima when she was younger but as time revealed her character he changed his mind, and when she took you out into the desert and assaulted you—' his strong face clenched hard '—he was quite appalled, as was I. She has agreed to marry a Saudi prince and I understand she is quite content. It was only ambition which made Fatima throw herself at me... I have never been more embarrassed in my thirty years of existence than I was that day, and that you should witness such a scene—'

'And misinterpret it in the most unkind way—'

'Cruelly unkind.' But he smiled that heart-stopping smile, and he took her mouth with drowning sweetness.

A loud knock landed on the door. With searing impatience Razul sprang off the bed. He had a short exchange with whoever had interrupted them, but when he turned back from the door he was smiling with amusement. He was holding the exquisite bonsai tree she had admired at the old palace.

'Such a gift from my father quite takes my breath away,' he confided. 'These trees are like his children.'

'You'd better give it back fast. All the leaves keep falling off the ones I have at home!' she admitted. 'They're hanging onto life by a slender thread.'

'Even better. He loves to instruct.'

'I'm frightened to death of him!' she gasped.

'But you must have impressed him deeply.' Razul gathered her back into his arms. 'Import the dying ones. They will be a challenge to him.'

He kissed her again.

'You know...I really do love you,' she whispered, glowing with contentment.

'But not enough to take me with two hundred concubines,' Razul lamented.

'You've got your hands full with me,' Bethany told him sternly.

'This is true...this is wonderfully true,' he agreed, covering her soft mouth again with his, drinking in her response with glorying pleasure. 'You divinely precious woman...I have one small confession to make...'

'Hmm?'

'The helicopter waiting to take you to the airport that day...had you climbed aboard it, it would have suffered mechanical breakdown and failed as a means of transport.'

Her lashes fluttered.

'I had decided that half an hour was not long enough for you to make such a serious decision.'

'You had no intention of letting me go!' Bethany registered in a daze.

'I will never let go of my dream.'

Winding her into the strong circle of his arms, Razul suited his passionate embrace to the assurance, and the rising thunder of her heartbeat and the hot race of her pulse made her quite forget what she had been about to say. Instead she luxuriated in the wonderful feeling that she had finally come home.

HARLEQUIN  PRESENTS®

FROM HERE TO PATERNITY

men who find their way to fatherhood by fair means,
by foul, or even by default!

Maddie adored men, and had no intention of
marrying one, but she did so want children.

Miles MacMillan had all the qualities Maddie
wanted in the father of her child....

Maddie + Miles = baby?

Watch for:

#1884 MADDIE'S LOVE-CHILD

by

Miranda Lee

Available in May 1997 wherever
Harlequin books are sold.

HARLEQUIN  PRESENTS®

Popular author Penny Jordan has worked her magic on
three compelling romances, all complete stories in
themselves. Follow the lives of Claire, Poppy and Star in:

THE BRIDE'S BOUQUET

Three women make a pact to stay single,
but one by one they fall, seduced by the
power of love....

Claire is the first to walk down the aisle:
Brad Chandler is sure that beneath her calm exterior
lies a deep passion. Is he prepared to wait for
that passion to reveal itself?
And when it does...

#1883 WOMAN TO WED?

Available in May 1997 wherever
Harlequin books are sold.

LOVE *or* MONEY?
Why not Love *and* Money!
After all, millionaires need love, too!

How to Marry a MILLIONAIRE

Suzanne Forster, Muriel Jensen and Judith Arnold

bring you three original stories
about finding that one-in-a million man!

Harlequin also brings you
a million-dollar sweepstakes—enter
for your chance to win a fortune!

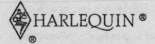

HARLEQUIN ®